Lynn stared.

Rick Branigan stood there the way he had on the first day she'd met him. Stubborn. Taciturn. And utterly unimpressed with the McCoys' billions.

The colonel gave a short nod. Decision made. "Well, I've only known this marine to make one mistake." He looked at her. "If he's doing what he thinks is best, I'll support him until he tells me to do otherwise."

Lynn gasped. The colonel was making the DUI hit-and-run sound like a brain burp, the same as shaking a salad dressing bottle without the lid on tight. But this was one colossal mess that Rick shouldn't be allowed to clean up on his own.

Especially when he was most likely innocent.

Dear Reader,

Honor, courage and commitment. Necessary ingredients in the making of a hero, as far as I'm concerned. And, not surprisingly, the central values of the United States Marine Corps. Personally, I believe a marine is one of the ultimate heroes—a man who is, by definition, always faithful.

He's the perfect man to pit against the billionaire McCoys as they try to quietly bring home the deceased Marcus McCoy's illegitimate prodigy in this third installment of THE LOST MILLIONAIRES series.

Major Rick Branigan is an exemplary marine until his faithfulness to an old friend threatens to cost him everything. The last thing he needs or wants is to become part of the McCoy dynasty.

Lynn Hayes, the corporate lawyer sent to extract the major from his troubles and escort him back to Dependable, Missouri, lives by the motto No Ties, No Limits. But nothing could be more limiting to her plans for a secure future than Rick's refusal to cooperate.

Only together can these two learn the true meaning of honor. Through the power of love, of course!

I'm always happy to hear from readers. Please visit me at www.leahvale.com.

Leah Vale

THE MARINE
Leah Vale

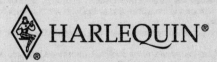

TORONTO • NEW YORK • LONDON
AMSTERDAM • PARIS • SYDNEY • HAMBURG
STOCKHOLM • ATHENS • TOKYO • MILAN • MADRID
PRAGUE • WARSAW • BUDAPEST • AUCKLAND

ISBN 0-373-75061-7

THE MARINE

Copyright © 2005 by Leah Vroman.

This edition published by arrangement with Harlequin Books S.A.

® and TM are trademarks of the publisher. Trademarks indicated with ® are registered in the United States Patent and Trademark Office, the Canadian Trade Marks Office and in other countries.

www.eHarlequin.com

Printed in U.S.A.

For Rod and Joan, the best in-laws a girl could ever hope for.
Not to mention shining examples of love and honor.

ACKNOWLEDGMENTS

Thank you to Orrin Grover for his legal advice
and willingness to play "what if?"

An extra-special thank-you to Colonel Al Arguedas,
USMC, Retired, for his knowledge, insight
and much-appreciated humor.

Any errors are the author's and probably on purpose.

Chapter One

Dear Major Branigan:

It is our duty at this time to inform you of the death of Marcus McCoy due to an unfortunate, unforeseen encounter with a grizzly bear while fly-fishing in Alaska on June 8 of this year, and per the stipulations set forth in his last will and testament, to make formal his acknowledgment of one USMC Major Rick Thomas Branigan, age 33, of 7259 Villa Crest Drive, #12, Oceanedge, California, as being his son and heir to an equal portion of his estate.

It is the wish of Joseph McCoy, father to Marcus McCoy, grandfather to Rick Branigan and founder of McCoy Enterprises, that you immediately assume your rightful place in the family home and business with all due haste and utmost discretion to preserve the family's privacy.

Regards,

David Weidman, Esq.

Weidman, Biddermier, Stark

"I don't have time for this right now," Major Rick Branigan grumbled at the letter he held in one hand while he braced his other hand against the open front door of his condo.

The lawyer lady on his doorstep looked around her, as if someone might actually hear them on the second-floor landing, then nodded sagely. "That's why I'm here, Major," she said in a rich, smooth voice straight out of a steamy, Southern-night fantasy.

Without being asked in, she brushed past Rick and entered his condo, as bold as you please.

She smelled faintly of an exotic spice that went perfectly with her amber eyes and winged black eyebrows but was as incongruent with her beige, don't-mess-with-me-in-court suit jacket and skirt as was her voice. Rick, in his lowly civi jeans and white T-shirt, turned to watch her stroll toward his glass-topped dining room table.

Her legs, as well as the rest of her, were shapely enough to win over any male jury. Not that he should be noticing, considering the latest complication heaped on his plate. But she was one hell of a looker despite the bun into which she'd pulled her black hair—one that would make a drill sergeant proud.

Only, he was no drill sergeant, and thanks to the felony charge he'd saddled himself with, he wouldn't be sitting on a jury anytime soon. His butt was likely destined for jail. He glanced out into the bright sunlight at the red pickup truck sitting in his parking space, its left front bumper and side panel bashed in. Damn, how had his life become so messed up so fast?

He shut the front door and followed her. "Excuse me, Ms….Hayes, was it?" He wasn't certain of her name because the fact that she was a lawyer for McCoy Enterprises, sent to hand-deliver a very special and wholly unexpected letter, had caught up his interest. Along with the contents of the letter. Rick waited to feel some emotional reaction to news of his father's death, but nothing came. He shrugged. He hadn't even known the guy's name.

The lawyer lady glanced up from where she was unloading papers from her sleek black leather brief-case. "That's correct. But please, call me Lynn. Especially since we'll be working closely for the next few days while I help represent you legally, then escort you to Dependable, Missouri."

Despite the sickening roll his stomach performed at her blithe mention of his need for legal representation, Rick scoffed. "I'm afraid you're mistaken about pretty much all of that, ma'am."

She paused, a file folder half out of her briefcase, and stared at him as if he'd just claimed women were better suited to working within the home—something his mother had single-handedly disproved.

"Mistaken?" She finished removing the file and placed it on the table with a telling deliberateness. "Major Branigan, I put forth a concerted effort to never make mistakes. They're counterproductive to my goals."

He eyed her courtroom version of spit-polish. The

woman seemed ready to argue a case before the Supreme Court, which seemed like overkill to him. Kind of like calling in a Harrier jet with full armament when a side arm would suffice. "Of which, I imagine, you have quite a few, Ms. Hayes."

"At the moment, just three. To quickly extract you from your current situation without drawing media attention and to get you to Dependable, Missouri, in time for your grandfather's seventy-fifth birthday party a month from now on July third."

"That's only two. What's the third?"

She froze. Without looking at him, she stated, "The third is personal, Major."

Personal, eh? What sort of personal goal would a clearly high-priced attorney have? She'd already been hired by one of the most successful general retail corporations in the United States, if not the world. McCoy stores were found everywhere and sold pretty much everything one needed in this modern world.

Wondering why she'd mention a third goal in the first place if it was personal, he fished. "But tied to the other two?"

"Yes," she crisply admitted. Then she added, "Now, let's review the facts of your case to ensure the information I was given is correct."

He clenched his abs against the anger and dread starting to party in his gut. "I'm not interested in you helping me prove my innocence, Ms. Hayes." Especially when she worked for his father's family.

"I'm *not* interested in helping you prove your innocence, Major. I'm here to facilitate a speedy and *un-*

noteworthy end to the situation you've found yourself
in. We need to plead you down to a lesser charge of
reckless driving—or best, failure to heed a traffic sig-
nal—instead of leaving you to face felony DUI hit-
and-run. Then getting you discharged will be simple.
Quick. Assuming the judge or magistrate and prosecutor are as agreeable as Joseph believes they will be
because of your record. Granted, since I'm not licensed
to practice law in the state of California, all I can do is
offer advice to the lawyer we hire for you—"

"I already have a lawyer." If only to speed up the
inevitable: demotion at best, dishonorable discharge
and prison at worst.

The anger and dread spread into his chest.

She shifted her weight, drawing his attention
briefly to the curve of her hip. "Forgive me, but I'm
not sure it'd be wise to retain council from—" she
flipped open the top file and read "—Acme Legal
Services." Her mouth flattened, as if the name tasted
bad. She studied him for a moment. "Please don't tell
me you picked the first firm listed in the phone book."

So what if he had? Since he'd been pleading the
Fifth nearly from the get-go, the quality of his lawyer didn't matter. Still, he wished the man hadn't automatically submitted a plea of not guilty at the
arraignment hearing.

Rick looked her in the eyes and crossed his arms
over his chest by way of answer.

She made a save-me-from-idiots noise as she
pulled out a chair—the one at the head of the table—
and sat down. Unconsciously or not, the woman

knew how to send a message. She was the independent, in-charge type. His mother would love her.

Another reason to have nothing to do with her.

Sliding the open file in front of herself, Ms. Hayes produced a hefty black-and-gold pen from her briefcase. "Arranging for new council will be the first order of business."

"No."

Her pen stilled on her notepad. Without glancing at him, she asked, "Care to explain why?" Her tone was casual enough, but a hint of mounting annoyance snuck through.

Some of the Marine officers he admired the most used a similar tactic to convey their opinions.

This admirable quality aside, he was in no mood to play today. Probably never would be again. "No. Nor do I care for your help." Though he'd done so inadvertently, he'd placed himself on this path and had every intention of reaching, with honor and dignity, whatever end it might hold for him.

Scrubbing a hand over his face, Rick fought the panic-spurred temptation to let her help him. "It's time for you to leave, Ms. Hayes."

"Major Branigan." She carefully set her pen on a file that undoubtedly contained everything about him down to his regulation shoe size.

Everything but the truth.

Folding her hands in front of her, she stared at him, her amber eyes glowing with conviction. "I understand the need to accept punishment for getting into your truck and driving after having a six-pack too many beers—especially considering the extent of the injuries the woman in the car you hit suffered." She glanced at the file. "One Emelie Dawson, forty-six, divorced mother of two. But I refuse to allow you to offer yourself up that way."

He remembered the letter he still gripped, and looked at it again. "Because that would be bad for the McCoys?"

Her response was unapologetic. "Because it would be bad for the McCoys."

He shouldn't care, shouldn't want to know after all this time. But he couldn't stop himself from finding out more about his father's family.

He asked, "Isn't making known their connection to me—and the circumstances surrounding it—worse? I recall seeing a fluffy report about the McCoys on one of those entertainment news shows. The reporter said the head of the family is some sort of high-moral-standards drum banger. Revealing that one of his kids—"

"Marcus was Joseph's only child."

Rick frowned. "His only—? Granted, the reporter was some ex–beauty queen, but I could have sworn she mentioned—"

"Alexander McCoy is actually Marcus's first illegitimate child," she smoothly interrupted him again.

So smoothly it took him a moment to register what she'd conveyed in that honey-slick voice of hers.

"I'm not his only?"

"No. You're one of four men."

"Four!" His already low opinion of the man who'd sired him crashed and burned.

He had three half siblings. But they would never be the brothers to him that his fellow Marines were.

The lady lawyer coolly shifted the file in front of her. "While my purpose here is to—"

"I know what your damn purpose is, Ms. Hayes," he said, doing some interrupting of his own, but not nearly as smoothly as she had. The story he'd thought he'd known was turning out to be even worse. He might as well have it all. "But the only thing I want from you is what you know about my father."

LYNN HAYES COULD ONLY stare at the compelling, seething man standing stiffly before her, his hands fisted at his sides, the letter he should have considered his salvation crumpled in one big, strong hand. His reaction to not only the letter but to her presence stunned her. She didn't like being stunned, and she needed every ounce of her self-control not to let the unwelcome feeling show. She couldn't afford to mess this up. Everything she'd worked so hard for to this point depended on success.

She looked back down at the file she'd acquired from the base commander—Joseph McCoy's connections never ceased to amaze and inspire—that detailed a military career epitomizing United States Marine Corps values. Major Rick Branigan had been awarded several medals, including a Purple Heart for injuries sustained in the first days of full-scale military action in Afghanistan. Injuries that, while in no way debilitating, now kept him from combat assignments but hadn't made him want out.

By all accounts, Major Branigan was indeed one of the best and the brightest, having achieved his current rank mere months ago and having had a spotless record, even before joining the Corps.

So why would he throw it all away by driving drunk, then fleeing the scene of an accident he'd caused?

Some people—people like her parents—just didn't realize how good they had it. They cared only for the buzz of the moment. Then, when they finally screwed up big and had everything taken away, they could only stand there with blank looks on their faces.

Only, Major Branigan didn't have a blank look on his handsome face. His classic McCoy features—strong jaw, aristocratic nose (though he had clearly busted his at one time) and arresting, deep blue eyes—radiated emotions he was visibly trying to contain. Emotions that were at odds with the Marine Corps poster boy he'd first appeared to be—complete with the Corps's emblem tattooed on his bulging left biceps.

Definitely not the one Lynn had expected. Personally, she would have given anything to find out she didn't really belong to the family she'd been born into. A family devoid of love and support. But she couldn't blame him for wanting to hear about his connection to the McCoys rather than about what she could do for him.

Still, she hesitated. "I'm not sure it's my place to tell you what I know about the Lost Millionaires." She wasn't one of the McCoys' advisors. Yet.

His rigid stance collapsed under the weight of his incredulity. "Lost Millionaires?"

"That's what Joseph called you all while coordinating efforts to track you down after learning of your existence when Marcus's will was read last Wednesday, June twelfth."

His eyes slid closed. "Just tell me."

She refolded her hands. "While none of this is for public consumption, mind you—"

"Imagine that."

"Yes, well…"

He opened his eyes, and she fought the unusual urge to squirm beneath his hard, blue gaze.

Something furry brushed against her bare shin and made her jump. She glanced down in time to see a cat in the guise of a small ring-tailed lemur, its eyes as startlingly blue as its owner's, cozying up to her. "You have a cat."

"Yes, I have a cat."

Momentarily derailed by the reality of a macho military type like him owning something so…fluffy, she just stared at it. It stared back.

"You were saying?" Major Branigan's deep voice returned her focus.

She shifted her leg out of the way and met his equally inscrutable stare. "Apparently, Marcus McCoy indulged in several short-lived, clandestine relationships that resulted in children being born— all boys thus far, interestingly enough—"

"And he paid each mother a million dollars to keep the identity of her illegitimate baby's father a secret, even from the kids themselves, right? Or was my mother simply a better negotiator than the rest when it came to her 'consulting fee'?"

The pain in his sharp tone made her stomach tighten.

"No—" Lynn was forced to clear her throat against her unexpected and unprecedented empathy. Why in the heck should she feel for him? His mom had scored herself a butt-load of security.

All *her* mother had ever scored was her next high— Lynn blinked to cut off the thought and refocus. *No ties, no limits.*

She lifted her chin. "No," she repeated. "All the women were paid the same sum and given the same conditions."

His stance relaxed almost imperceptibly. "And this Alexander McCoy...?"

"Actually the maid's son. Raised by the McCoys to believe he was Marcus's brother."

"So much for the McCoy stores' motto—'Don't trust it if it's not from the real McCoy.'"

Worried about the distaste in his voice, she nodded slowly.

"Unbelievable. At least my mom was always straight up with me about the circumstances surrounding why my father wanted to remain anonymous and where the money she'd used to start her architecture firm had come from." He shook his fist holding the letter, eyeing it. "Admirable bunch."

The McCoys were, but Lynn let his sarcasm pass and simply lifted a shoulder. What he thought of them wasn't her concern.

"What about the other two guys?"

"One is a rancher in Colorado. The other, a contractor, lives in Dependable and was easy to contact." Because he, too, had managed to land his rear in jail, Lynn had discovered when she'd checked in after arriving here. Merely a charge for disorderly conduct, and easily resolved. Something she'd hoped the major's would be, too.

Determined to make it so, she continued. "Joseph had hoped to notify you all simultaneously, but I was delayed in getting all the pertinent information I need surrounding your case. We thought it best for me to have everything before contacting you."

Thank goodness the next phase in his hearing process was also delayed because of a clogged court docket and the fact the primary witness—the driver in the car he hit—couldn't be present yet. The woman was stuck in a hospital bed, in traction. Unfortunate for the woman, but it bought Lynn time. Time she apparently was going to require.

Relaxing his grip, he uncrumpled the paper. "So why name his sons in his will and blow the family-secrets closet wide open?"

"Joseph believes Marcus finally saw the error of his ways."

Branigan raised his gaze to hers. "Did you know this Marcus?"

"Yes. He frequently worked with those of us in Legal preparing contracts for suppliers or for developers who wanted the McCoys to open new stores. Though more often than not, he teleconferenced or e-mailed because he was usually off somewhere handling client relations."

"And now everyone knows the sort of 'handling' he liked to do." The major gave her a quick once-over, his meaning clear in his sharp eyes.

Lynn kept her mouth shut. While she'd caught Marcus looking a little too long at her breasts and legs and he had always indulged in mild flirtation with her—as well as with a lot of other women at McCoy Enterprises—things had never progressed further. He'd either learned his lesson, or he'd considered her and the other ladies to be too close to home. He *had* left one other woman from Dependable, besides the maid, pregnant and rich but that woman had been the last of his fertile flings.

They hoped.

The major reread the letter. "Seems he didn't have very good relations with grizzly bears."

"Apparently."

He looked her dead in the eye. "So why do *you* think he claimed us—the 'Lost Millionaires'—in his will? Especially after going to such expense years ago to cut himself loose from his duty and responsibility?"

Lynn didn't blink. "I can't begin to speculate."

Oh, but she had. Endlessly. And she had her theories. None of which she was going to share with the man she'd been sent to bring into the McCoy fold without scandal.

Marcus realizing the error of his ways certainly wasn't one of her theories. Nor was guilt. That wasn't his style—even if he'd placed his illegitimate sons in his will because he fully expected to live a lot longer than he had, a reasonable assumption on his part considering how robust Joseph still was at nearly seventy-five years of age.

Major Branigan tossed the letter onto the table. "Doesn't matter why. I'm not going to be attending some family reunion anytime soon." He turned and walked to the tall windows in his attractively decorated living room with its view of the distant ocean.

He was so tall and well shaped beneath his white T-shirt and jeans that Lynn had to admit she preferred the view she had from where she sat. Which was saying something, because she sure as heck wasn't a card-carrying member of the Pocket Watchers of America.

She'd never even spoken with the girls who'd wasted their time checking out the back pockets of the boys' Levi's in school. Her focus was normally on her schooling or work. But the major *was* work.

Fortunately, the tension radiating from every lean, hard inch of the man squashed any pleasure that checking out his butt might have given her.

The breadth of his shoulders expanded as he inhaled deeply, then slowly exhaled. "Even if I were free to leave town, I still wouldn't be interested. I'm a Marine, ma'am."

"Not for long if you're convicted. I'm sure you're well aware of the fact that you'll be dishonorably discharged before you can say 'ooh-rah.'"

His hands fisted at his sides again. "That's *hoo-rah*. And what happens to me is none of your business."

"Your grandfather, Joseph McCoy, has made it my business. He's not about to let a grandson he's just found out about go to jail if he doesn't have to." An attitude that had shocked her, given Joseph's morally upstanding reputation.

The major turned slowly to face her, his jaw hardened with the sort of determination only a decade in the Marines could give a man. "I said yes when the cops asked if I was driving that truck the night of the accident. I'm afraid Mr. McCoy is out of luck."

Her knee-jerk response was *Not if I can help it,* but something about his admission of guilt struck her as odd. Coupled with what she knew about him from his files…

The fine hairs on her arms stood on end. Something was wrong. *Did Joseph suspect as much, also? Was that why he was willing to seek special treatment for the first time that she was aware of?*

She shook her intuition off. She wasn't here to worry about right or wrong. She was here to earn the promotion Joseph had all but promised her in exchange for the presence of this grandson at his birthday party on July third. The promotion could be one more step upward. One more step toward the security she could never be too sure of.

Her third goal—a security for which she'd do anything, sacrifice anything.

Chapter Two

"You should have more faith in my abilities, Major Branigan."

"Your abilities are not in question, Ms. Hayes." Though Rick had tried to keep his attention fixed on the distant view of the late-morning sun glinting off the Pacific Ocean, his body was all too aware of the woman seated behind him. His gaze strayed from the older apartment complex down the hill from his condominium to his smashed red pickup truck sitting out front.

What had Pete been thinking?

But that was just it. Pete didn't think; he simply *did.* Always had. When they were kids, Rick, as Pete's best friend, had been there to divert disaster. A lot had changed between them since, yet not everything.

Needing to move, to *do* something, he turned from the window and headed for the door. Nothing more than a symbolic way out, but at the moment, he'd take anything he could get.

"What is in question is how we're going to— Major Branigan?" she practically yelled.

He glanced back at her as he yanked open the front door. Her exotic eyes were wide. For the first time since she'd strolled through his door she looked flustered, no longer the queen of her domain.

Normally, he would have felt guilty about being so rude, but he'd stowed his conscience the day the cops had come knocking.

He was about to step out—

"Major!"

He relented and made up an excuse to toss her. "I have to work on my truck." He reached back in and scooped his keys off the small table in the hall. "Just be sure you shut the door behind you after you've gathered your stuff. Don't want Buddy to get out." He pointed at the cat beneath the table, watching him with blatant interest. Rick never knew what the damn thing was going to do from one minute to the next.

The lawyer glanced from the cat, to her files, to him, opening and closing her mouth as if wanting to sputter but too polished to actually indulge in something so telling. Rick took advantage of her distress and left the condo, shutting the door behind him.

He'd barely made the landing before he heard his door open and close quickly—good, no escape for Buddy today, the slippery cat—then her heels rapped on the stairs as she hurried down.

"Major Branigan—"

His attention on finding the key to his storage closet at the back of the carport, he called, "Thank you for delivering that letter, Ms. Hayes." He passed his tarp-covered Suzuki motorcycle and when he heard her walk up behind him, he added, "At least now I know my father's name."

It didn't change the way he felt about the man, or how he intended to live his life. Duty bound and with honor. All the way to the ugly end.

"Major. *Rick*."

Her imploring use of his name made him glance at her as he opened the storage closet. She visibly clenched her jaw while she stared at him, single file folder gripped in her hands, marring her smooth, perfectly sculpted face.

This one didn't back down. He liked that. But with him, such tenacity wouldn't help her get what she wanted. Her three goals—whatever the third one was—would not be achieved.

Mustering as much finality and sincerity as he could, he said, "It was nice meeting you, Ms. Hayes."

She studied him for a moment. Rick had the distinct impression he was being searched, that she was trying to see through him to the truth of him. To the sort of man he really was.

Wouldn't do her any good. That man had been sacrificed to repay a debt.

He turned away and reached into the closet for his tool kit. When he straightened, she was reading the papers within the folder she had balanced open in one hand.

She mused, "So you admitted guilt to the arresting officers—"

He shut the storage-closet door. "We've already covered that."

She ran a finger across a page. "But you refused any form of testing for blood-alcohol levels despite repeated warnings that doing so would be used against you at trial, and you refused further questioning."

He narrowed his eyes at her. "How do you know what I refused?"

"I have a copy of the police report right here."

"How did you get that?"

A finely shaped black brow twitched. "The McCoys are remarkably connected, Major."

"You mean rich enough to buy what they need."

She slowly raised her eyes to his. "Actually, based on my experience during the five years I've worked for McCoy Enterprises, people are often eager to do things for the McCoys." She shrugged. "Whether out of hope for future business opportunities or simply to be able to say they've had personal dealings with billionaires."

Not interested in either of those things, and not caring to have his life bared for perusal by anyone except the military, he shifted the large, red metal toolbox to his other hand. "What else do you have there?"

Her smile was supremely confident. "I have it all, so you might as well accept the fact that I'm here to help you. I didn't come all the way from Missouri for nothing."

"No way, Ms. Hayes." He turned and headed out of the carport.

She followed, her strides remarkably long and determined despite the height of her heels and the snugness of her skirt. Which were two things he hadn't wanted to notice, given the disaster his life had become. So he stopped and asked, "Or is it 'Mrs.'? Don't you have a husband or someone waiting on you? Why don't you fly home early and surprise him, ma'am."

She made a disgusted-sounding noise. "Afraid not, Major. It's *Miss,* and even if it weren't, even if there was someone waiting for me to come home, which there isn't, he'd just have to wait." She glared for several moments, then her expression softened and she shifted toward him.

His survival-training-honed instincts went on high alert.

In a beguiling tone that was a far better match to her unusual eyes and full mouth, she said, "On the other hand, the more you cooperate with me, the sooner we can get you free of this unpleasantness. And the sooner you're free of this unpleasantness, the sooner you can be rid of me. So it's entirely up to you, Major."

It was Rick's turn to make a disgusted sound as he started again toward his truck. He might free himself of her, but they both knew he'd never be free of the stain "this unpleasantness" would leave on his reputation.

Nor would he be free of the McCoys, for that matter. His mood darkened further. He wasn't about to run to them because he had nothing else to do.

He dropped his toolbox with a bang next to the crushed left front of the once dingless Dodge.

Planting his hands on his hips, he tried to ignore the woman next to him by focusing on the truck's damage. The lights on this side were completely obliterated, the hood had buckled and the side panel was creased and streaked with black paint.

From the other car. The car of Emelie Dawson, forty-six, divorced mother of two.

If only he'd looked closer that night, he would have realized a tree hadn't caused the damage. His throat tightened and his stomach turned.

Focus on what you have power over.

He examined the front of the truck. He'd have to pry the bumper away from the wheel to keep from further trashing the tire if he wanted to drive the truck to the repair shop rather than have it towed— a minor concession he'd make to his restrained pride. There'd be a little too much symbolism involved in having to watch his truck being winched up onto a flatbed and hauled away.

He pushed the button on the key fob and unlocked the truck so he could get a crowbar from the space in back of the seat.

Behind him, *Miss* Hayes said, "I'm surprised they didn't impound your vehicle."

"They did. My *Acme* lawyer got it returned to me right after the police processed it."

Without commenting, she said crisply, "Back to the police report. You initially admitted to having driven this truck the night of the accident. Is that correct?"

Rick stifled a sigh as he backed out of the cab and

straightened, crowbar in hand. Maybe if he let her see exactly how little help she could provide, she'd leave. He shut the truck's door. "Correct."

He'd said the words that night; now he'd pay the price.

She moved just enough to let him get down on the blacktop to search beneath the bumper for a good leverage point. "But then you exercised your Fifth Amendment right to remain silent in order to avoid incriminating yourself. Why? Why not just ask to speak with an attorney before you answered any more questions?"

He found a notched spot and fit one end of the crowbar against it, then braced the other one on the bumper. "Because talking to a lawyer then wouldn't have made any difference. I still wasn't going to answer any questions."

"Because you're guilty."

He grunted an answer, but the acceptance in her tone made him shove on the wedged crowbar extra hard.

"Okay, then. Let's walk through the facts."

"I don't want your help, Miss Hayes."

"Humor me. And please, call me Lynn."

She was cozying up to him, to get him to let her into the game. The healthy male in him locked and loaded at the mere thought of cozying up to a looker like her—but no way.

"Witnesses have you leaving the Rancho Margarita Bar's parking lot in a truck matching the description of this one—"

She stepped close and lightly kicked the tire next

to his shoulder with her beige, high heeled shoe. She wasn't wearing any hose, and her incredibly smooth, lightly tanned skin pulled his gaze upward over a slender ankle, a toned calf, a perfect knee, a satiny thigh shadowed by the hem of her skirt…

"—and heading south in the northbound lane for approximately a hundred yards before making a correction." She humphed and shifted her weight. "Hard to claim a momentary lapse of control caused the accident."

Rick jerked his attention back to the crowbar, practically forgotten in his hands. "That it would be," he concurred, pretending that he hadn't just been peering up her skirt. He knew the perspiration forming on his back and his forehead said otherwise.

He gave the crowbar a fast, hard push.

She shifted again, but this time he only allowed himself a glance. Damn, but she had nice legs. Runner's legs. The kind that had to be earned, especially since she appeared to be about his age. Thirty-something women didn't keep legs like that free.

He gritted his teeth and pushed again. The bumper moved an inch with a satisfying metal-on-metal *squawk*.

"Why don't you just let them crank the thing up on a flatbed and haul it to a shop?"

"Because." He grumbled and pushed at the bumper a third time. "It's not that bad."

She scoffed. "If you say so. But according to this, you must have been traveling about thirty miles per hour when you ran the light after getting into the right lane. No skid marks before you hit the black sedan as it was starting its left-hand turn. Just because you could back up and drive away doesn't mean your truck isn't trashed."

She took a step nearer and he glanced up to see her peering into the cab. "Ah. So that's what an airbag looks like. Can't be easy to drive with all that hanging out of the steering wheel into your lap. Or feel pleasant when it nails you."

Good thing he had no intention of taking his shirt—or anything else—off around this woman, because she was certain to spot that he didn't have a mark on him other than his tattoo.

"Too bad the airbag in the car you hit couldn't prevent the driver from getting her pelvis broken. I can't imagine anything that would hurt worse."

He grunted in response, using all his strength to shove the bumper outward, away from the wheel well so the tire could turn freely. He didn't want to think about the specifics of that night, didn't want to form a picture that would play over and over in his head. The future held enough nightmares for him as it was.

But he was a man of his word, and he'd given his word. Besides, now it was all too late.

"Interesting."

He paused, only barely refraining from asking *what?*

"It says here, you refused a breathalyzer and blood test at the station, but exhibited no signs of inebriation. Even though they were able to track you down within the hour from the partial plate number the victim noted as you were backing away and the fact that you were holding a beer when you opened the door. Care to comment?"

"Nope." Man, he'd needed a beer after taking one look at Pete.

"Didn't think so."

She didn't sound thwarted at all. Or even perturbed. She sounded intrigued, like a woman unwilling to butt out.

Not good. Not good at all.

THE LATE-MORNING SUN glared off the papers within the folder and made Lynn too warm in her suit coat. Still, she stood there next to the truck and read through the rest of the faxed copy of the police report, using far more care than she had the first time in her hotel suite while familiarizing herself with the case after she'd finally received all the documentation. Now that she'd met the soon-to-be-ex-Major Rick Branigan, different things were jumping out at her. Things that didn't make sense. Things that were making her instincts go nuts.

While she was no defense attorney or any kind of a trial lawyer, she didn't get to work for McCoy Enterprises's Legal because she was just good at contracts. She'd worked her tail off at the University of Missouri and Columbia Law to be the best of the best. A regular G.I. Jane of law up against all the Ivy League grads. Her instincts had yet to fail her, and she'd learned to trust them.

Once again she squinted through the dirty driver's window at the deflated airbag, very much like a big white balloon that had been popped and forgotten. Then she realized the window wasn't dirty on the outside, but coated with residue left by the powder from the airbag. Drivers often had burns as well as bruises and abrasions on their arms and faces from an airbag's violent inflation.

She looked down at the mile of man stretched out at her feet. No sign of injury of any kind, old or new. Just muscle, sinew and a bullheadedness she might normally have respected.

The copy of the mug shot in the file she'd barely glanced at earlier—she'd simply registered a McCoy family resemblance then—was of a disturbingly handsome face marred only by a heartbreaking stoicism. It was the face of a man prepared to give nothing but name, rank and serial number.

She searched through the police report for any indication that he'd had injuries from the accident or bore evidence of taking an airbag in the kisser, which, for whatever reason, wasn't visible in his picture. She didn't find anything.

She knew drunks often walked away from horrific wrecks without serious injury because their bodies were so relaxed that the jolt of the impact didn't harm them. But she doubted being relaxed would save someone from the punishment that an early-model airbag—which this truck surely had—could dole out.

She chewed on her lip for a minute. Branigan was

tall. His chest could have taken the brunt of the force. She could ask him to remove his shirt so she could check for bruises… A trickle of sweat ran down between her breasts.

Instead, she asked, "Have you done laundry lately, Major?"

He paused in his battle with the bumper and squinted up at her. "What?"

The guy had nice teeth. Among other things. "I was just wondering if you'd washed the clothes you were wearing the night of the accident."

He went very still. "Why?"

"Because I'd like to see them."

"Why?" he repeated, but with even more suspicion.

"To check if there's residue on them from the airbag. The same stuff that's all over the inside of your truck."

He squinted up at her for a moment more, then used his strong leg to push himself farther beneath the bumper. "Sorry. Laundry day was yesterday."

Liar.

She had no idea why she was so certain, but she was. And he had no reason to lie to her. He knew his guilt or innocence didn't matter to her. If he didn't want her to see his clothes because he didn't want her help, he could just tell her no.

So why lie to her? Unless he was lying about other things… Or copping the Fifth to avoid having to lie…

She snapped the folder closed and leaned her shoulder against the side mirror. "So what were you celebrating?"

"Celebrating?"

"Yes, celebrating. There was nothing in your files about any sort of drinking problem, so you must have been celebrating something to tie one on like that."

More clanking, more protesting metal. "Guess it'd been a good day."

"A good day? Hmm." She flipped to another page in the file. "Let's see. It says your MOS is 0302. What does that mean?"

There was a long silence, and just as she was deciding he wasn't going to answer, he said, "MOS stands for Military Occupational Specialty, and 0302 is Infantry."

She already knew as much, having spent several late hours the night before she flew out to California poring over the USMC's Web site. By the time she finished, *she'd* wanted to join up. But she needed to draw him out.

"Thank you. I imagine you form quite a few strong bonds in the infantry. So who were you with? You know, at the bar? Who were you drinking with?"

Silence from beneath the truck.

Lynn's confidence in her gut instinct grew. "Or were you drinking alone? The witnesses said there'd been just one person in the red pickup. And if you'd been with friends, they wouldn't have been very good friends to let you get into your truck and drive away drunk enough not to recognize your right from your left. So were you at the Rancho Margarita Bar drinking alone?"

While she didn't expect one, she gave time for an answer.

When enough time had passed, she continued. "Though the cops wouldn't have bothered checking, because you're making their job easy as hell, I'm sure the bartender will remember you. Definitely the cocktail waitresses. I mean, a guy like you—" She caught herself before she elaborated on his very memorable traits.

No need to let him know she found him attractive. She was there simply to get him out of this potential disaster with the civilian authorities and have him discharged from the Marines fast.

She straightened away from the side mirror. If there was more to this story—namely, that Major Rick Branigan hadn't been driving this truck when it plowed into another car—then she could either get him free of the charges quickly, or she'd end up dragging the investigation out for months. Especially if he continued to behave like a jackass and withhold his cooperation.

Considering the clock always ticking in the back of her mind and what she had at stake, did she dare risk finding out?

Chapter Three

"What do you mean, a guy like me?"

His speculative tone from beneath the truck snapped Lynn out of her dire musings. She realized the major wasn't wrenching on the bumper anymore.

Still conflicted over what she wanted to do about his potential innocence, she tried for a casual approach, as if she were stating the obvious. "The type waitresses remember."

"Which is?"

"Are you looking for compliments, Major?"

"Only if you're in the mood to give them, Miss Hayes."

What she was in the mood for was an open-and-shut case. A case that wouldn't give her a moment's pause but would earn her one more notch in her belt. One more promotion to insulate her from the numbing chill of her past. One more reason to be able to sleep at night. If she shut down her instincts about his innocence right here, right now, this case could garner her the security she craved.

But could even *she,* a woman perfectly willing to

dart in front of a more tenured co-worker to get the next promotion, let an innocent man plead guilty to anything to get him where he needed to be on time? Could she sacrifice him for her own selfish needs?

The man in question pulled himself from beneath the truck and eyed her. "I was beginning to think you'd left."

She hadn't. She couldn't.

"Just searching for a suitable compliment."

He snorted and pushed himself to his feet. "If you have to try that hard, then don't bother."

Surprised by his sense of humor, she laughed. He stared at her, his brows raised. She did her best to ignore the fact that the man had beautiful eyes. "What?"

It was as though her question startled him back into action, and he brushed off the seat of his jeans and the back of his T-shirt. "I have to admit I didn't take you for the laughing sort."

Surprised at herself for being susceptible to him in any way, she raised her chin. "Sorry to disappoint you, Major."

"Trust me, I'm not disappointed." But he didn't sound happy, either. "I'll walk you up to my place so you can get the rest of your stuff."

So he was back to trying to get rid of her. Fine. She was ready to go. She had some serious thinking to do.

Lynn held up a hand. "That's okay. I can manage on my own. You stay down here so your tools don't go for a walk, too."

He turned his attention back to the truck. Planting his hands on his hips, he blew out a breath. "I still have my work cut out for me with this thing."

"Do you have something against body shops?"

His gaze flicked over her in a way that made her very conscious of her own body. In particular, what lay between her hem and the modest neckline of her buttoned blazer. Another bead of sweat erupted from the overheated skin at the top of her cleavage and started its slow progression down to her bra.

He met her eyes again. "Not a thing. But since the main base pool is closed today, I've nothing better to do."

"Are you a swimmer?" She couldn't help taking another visual inventory of his body. Thick biceps—with that eagle-globe-and-anchor tattoo that drew the eye—muscle-capped shoulders and strong-looking chest and legs. All of which she'd automatically attributed to his being in the military.

"All Marines are amphibious, ma'am." His delivery was deadpan, but the teasing light in his deep blue eyes derailed her for a second. He was joking.

Her look must have mirrored the one he'd given her after she'd laughed, because he raised his eyebrows again and said, "What?"

"I didn't take you for the joking sort."

"Sorry to disappoint, ma'am."

They exchanged a silent acknowledgment that there was more to each other than either had first thought.

Terrific. Lynn's heart started to pound.

The major widened his stance and crossed his

arms over his chest. "But I'd be at the pool because I was relieved of my normal duties and temporarily reassigned to Recreational Aquatics Thermal Regulator."

She didn't have the chance to ask for clarification before he provided it.

"I have to check the pool temperature every hour."

"Really."

"It was either that or handing out basketballs in the gym."

She winced. Talk about humiliating for a major to be reduced to such menial duties. And while it beat the heck out of sitting in jail, why in heaven's name wouldn't he want to be free of being the pool boy?

He watched her with his jaw jutted, clearly daring her to pity him.

Lynn contained the twinges of exactly that emotion by gripping the file folder to her chest. She cleared her throat. "Well, I'll leave you to your repairs while I go grab my briefcase and files."

He studied her, then gave a short nod. "Just be careful of the cat. Make sure it doesn't bolt out the door."

No worries there. The only one who'd be bolting out the door would be her.

"I'll keep an eye out for it." She turned away, then stopped. "Um, what's its name?" Why she'd thought to ask, let alone care, was beyond her. She wasn't the fuzzy-creature type. She wasn't *any* creature type.

"Bud."

"As in a flower or the beer?"

His mouth quirked. "As in Buddy."

A masculine name from a masculine guy. Still didn't make the cat any less fuzzy.

She nodded in acknowledgment and headed for the stairs to his second-story condo, her brain unnaturally sluggish given the choice she'd have to make.

If she could keep him out of jail, there would be nothing to prevent him from coming with her to Dependable.

If he pleaded guilty or she finagled the lesser charge and he paid the fine, the Marine Corps would be glad to be rid of him and she could give Joseph what he wanted, and he in turn would give her what *she* wanted.

But what if Rick Branigan was innocent?

She'd told him she didn't care about his innocence or guilt, but she'd lied. She'd once been innocent and had had to pay the price for someone else's actions. An injustice that had festered deep in her chest.

Lynn tucked the file folder under her arm and rubbed at one temple in an attempt to clear her thinking as she climbed the stairs. When she reached the major's door, she opened it and entered quickly to keep the cat from escaping. She scanned the room as she latched the door behind her. *Buddy* was sitting on the glass-topped dining-room table, smack-dab in the middle of her files, and looking very much in control of his world.

A personal challenge if she ever saw one.

Lynn marched to the table. "Get off, cat."

Not so much as a blink in response.

She picked up her briefcase and jammed the file containing the police report inside.

The cat stood, but only to stretch, raising his fluffy rear end in the air and digging his claws into her folders and papers. Lynn planted a fist on her hip and waited for him to finish. Once the claws were back in, she snatched a couple of the bottom files out from under him.

Buddy wasn't impressed.

She muttered, "Stupid cat."

The black phone on the kitchen bar rang, and they both jumped, Buddy off the table and Lynn back a step.

The phone rang again, and she glanced at the closed front door, wondering if she should let the major know he had a call. After the third ring and before she could decide, the answering machine kicked on and Rick Branigan's voice, just as deep and compelling as it was in person, announced that he was out and instructed the caller to leave a message.

No "How's it hanging?" or even "Hi," but not rude, either. Just to the point, without embellishment. The man would not be an easy one to figure out.

She shouldn't want to try.

The machine beeped and a woman's voice filled the room. "Rick, honey, it's Mom. You realize, don't you, that it's been ages since we talked. I called the base and all they would tell me was that you were unavailable. So, to keep from worrying about you, I've been convincing myself your answering machine must be broken." A telling pause. "If you get this, please call me. And even if you don't get this, you should still be checking in with your mother more often than this. The way you normally do."

The woman was clearly striving to be light and joking, but there was a definite undertone of fear.

"I love you. Bye."

Lynn stared at the blinking red light, the simple endearment making the backs of her eyes burn. Lynn would never have received a message like that from her mother, even if she were still in her life. It'd been years since the longing for family had been this bad.

Feeling ambushed, she swept the rest of the files into her briefcase with a careless hand and turned toward the door.

His mom didn't know.

The thought stopped Lynn. She forced herself to consider. Why hadn't he told his mother that his career, and freedom, were on the line? Because he didn't want to face his mother's disappointment?

Lynn shook her head. No. He struck her as the type who'd take it on the chin, sobbing momma or not. So why was he putting off the inevitable?

Because he doesn't want to be talked out of doing what he's doing.

The specter of his innocence rose again and made her conscience shudder. She shoved the uncomfortable sensation aside.

Maybe Major Branigan might find it easy to tell a stranger to go take a flying leap, but ignoring his mother's pleas to make the best of the situation and get on with his life was another thing.

Hopefully, he'd be willing to get on with his life under the protective wing of the McCoys in Dependable, Missouri.

An idea bloomed in Lynn's head and a renewed sense of determination surged through her with a power she'd come to depend upon.

She had no choice but to do anything she could to get Major Branigan in Dependable by July third.

Even if his momma had to drag him there.

WAITING IN HER hotel's sunny, tropical-themed coffee shop the next morning for Ann Branigan to arrive, Lynn stared at the concentric rings of white that the cream formed as she poured the thick liquid into her coffee. She'd already dumped in the contents of two packets of sweetener.

She used to not allow herself the luxury of making what she considered a nasty drink more palatable, worried that she might be perceived as less tough somehow for not taking her coffee strong and black. But after meeting with such steady success at McCoy Enterprises, she'd lightened up a bit. She swirled her spoon around the cup until the coffee was a pale brown.

Maybe she'd lightened up too much.

Was that why she was having such a hard time sticking with her original neutrality regarding the major's innocence or guilt? And was that why she'd agreed to wait until his mother could fly down from San Francisco to meet with her in person and talk at length about her son?

Lynn blew out a breath at her own foolishness and pushed the cup and saucer toward the center of the table, bumping the slender vase and its little purple orchids to the side. She'd only accepted being put off by Ann Branigan—after first telling the woman everything *she* knew, including the details of Marcus McCoy's will—because it had become plain to Lynn less than two minutes into the conversation that the major's mother was a woman to reckon with.

Ms. Branigan had not been happy to discover she'd been outed, that the secret she'd kept for so long was no longer a secret.

Thanks to the files Joseph McCoy's lawyers and private investigators had compiled after the reading of Marcus McCoy's will naming the women he'd paid off, Lynn had already known that Ms. Branigan was the owner of a very successful architectural design firm. Which was also how Lynn had known to get ahold of her. But Lynn had had no idea how strong a personality the woman would have.

Ms. Branigan had refused to give Lynn any insight into her son until they had a chance to meet face-to-face. Apparently holding on to a million-dollar secret for thirty-three years made her play things dang close to the vest.

But the major's mom had promised in exchange not to see Rick or talk to him until after that meeting.

She'd better not. Lynn needed her firmly in the get-this-over-quick-and-quiet camp before Ms. Branigan spoke with her son.

And then Lynn could put the specter of past wrongs and the moral consciousness he'd stirred in her to rest for good and go back to never thinking about what was over and done with. She wanted to think only about her future.

A bright one without shadows or fear.

The sound of wooden chair legs scraping on tile brought her out of her thoughts and her head up. An attractive, petite older woman with close-cropped brown hair was pulling out the chair across from Lynn. She wore a tailored leather jacket that matched her hair, over a tan blouse and slacks. A bright red scarf tied jauntily around her neck gave her a splash of color and style.

"Miss Hayes?" she asked, even though she'd clearly assumed she had the right table. Her smile was striking, but tight—so similar to her son's.

Lynn extended a hand. "Yes. And you must be Ann Branigan."

"I am." She slid into the seat with the ease of a woman used to breakfast meetings. The deep grooves on either side of her full mouth and her worry-clouded blue eyes made it obvious this was no regular business meeting to her. "Thank you for agreeing to meet with me."

"Thank you for flying down here." *Assuming you prove to be a help, not a hindrance.*

"How could I not?" She settled in and waved away the waitress and her coffeepot. "While he might not believe it, Rick is the most important part of my world."

Before Lynn could process the implications of Ms. Branigan's statement, she asked, "So tell me, how could this have happened? Who has Rick been mistaken for?"

Lynn blinked. His mother had automatically assumed him innocent, despite all the facts Lynn had relayed to her during their telephone conversation the night before.

Lynn's instincts reared up and shouted, *Ha, I told you so!* She stubbornly ignored them. "Ms. Branigan, your son confessed. Why would you think it's a mistake?"

"Please, call me Ann. And I'm positive there's been a mistake because I know my son, Miss Hayes."

"Lynn," she said, leveling the playing field. This woman was obviously the type who would cooperate only if she considered Lynn her equal.

Ann acknowledged her with a nod, then leaned forward, her round face radiating the strength of will her peppy attractiveness would normally belie. "Rick would never drive drunk, and he would never, *ever,* leave the scene of an accident, whether he caused it or not." She settled back again. "You see, Lynn, my son is all about duty and honor."

Lynn's spirits plummeted. So much for losing moral consciousness.

Through tight lips, she admitted, "I noticed."

"Hard not to. He lives and breathes the Marine code of honor, courage and commitment. Pretty much always has. When he was a teenager and found out that *Semper Fi* meant 'Always Faithful' he enlisted in the Marines' college-bound program the next day."

"Why?"

Ann inhaled deeply as she straightened the silverware in front of her. "When I asked him that very thing, he said he felt he had something to prove—whether to the world or himself, I'm not sure. What he didn't say—would never say, but it's something I've always known—is that he resents the choices his father and I made when I accidentally became pregnant."

"You and Marcus McCoy," Lynn clarified in a low voice.

"Yes. Neither of us wanted a long-term commitment. Marcus, understandably, didn't want his identity revealed. I agreed to his terms because I'd be able to secure my child's future by investing the money he was offering in my business. My hope had been that Rick would grow up and take over the company. He had different ideas. And I respect that."

Different ideas that would cost Lynn her chance for guaranteed security. "But now that his ideas about his future have been effectively demolished, will you help me convince him to take the easiest way out of the trouble he's in?"

"No."

Shock loosened Lynn's jaw, and she fought not to gape.

It must have shown, because Ann's expression softened and she leaned near. "Not because I don't want to, Lynn. But Rick—who I know loves me dearly—nevertheless deep down doesn't respect me. He doesn't realize that I'm aware of his feelings. And I believe that he struggles with them. But the truth is there in the choices he makes."

Ann's sigh held a mother's regret. "I've never been able to influence him. Fortunately, his choices are always ones that I can be proud of. Though they're not always in his best interest, as far as I'm concerned." She shook her head. "If he'd chosen to work for me he'd be very rich by now."

A gloominess stealing over Lynn, she muttered, "He already *is* very rich, thanks to the inheritance from his father. Very, *very* rich."

Ann slumped back. "I suppose he is." She shook her head again and tsked. "Poor Marcus. *A grizzly bear.* How awful."

Feeling as though there was a grizzly bear of her own slobbering down her neck, Lynn clarified. "So you don't believe you can convince Rick to accept my help or change his mind about this silent acceptance of whatever the punishment might be?"

"I wish I could. And I wish there was some hope that you could convince him yourself."

Lynn sat up straighter. "What makes you think I can't?"

"Because I can already tell that he's going to react to you the same way he reacts to me."

"Which is?"

"By doing the exact opposite of what you suggest."

Dread churned in Lynn's stomach like acid from the coffee she hadn't drunk. "Why?"

Ann's blue eyes glowed with certainty. "We're too much alike, you and I."

Lynn clenched her jaw. So she was on her own. Nothing new there. It appeared she'd have no choice but to discover the truth about Rick's accident.

Then she could decide what to do.

RICK DREW STRENGTH from his frustration and lifted the heavier-than-normal weights away from his sides, his hissing breath loud in the deserted fitness room across the parking lot from his condo. While he'd never really thought much about the convenience of having a place to exercise at his condominium complex because he normally worked out on base, he'd found it a godsend in the days since he'd been released on bail. He probably would have exploded with frustration had he not been able to release some of the steam as sweat that drenched his white sleeveless T-shirt and black shorts.

Today he could have given Hercules a good go. It was already midmorning, and he was still going strong.

He couldn't believe Lawyer Lady's gall—

The door leading out to the parking lot opened. "Ah, it *is* you."

Rick faltered and nearly dropped the dumbbells. *Man, now she's showing up when I think about her.* Talk about a reason to stop thinking about her.

He turned to find Lynn striding toward him. Though how she practically marched in those heels was beyond him. The pale blue color and feminine cut of her suit coat and matching pants screamed girly-girl, but her in-charge walk, tightly pulled back hair and set jaw belied the packaging.

She was an interesting contradiction. And *so* not for him.

He turned away and readjusted his hold on the weights. "Butt out of my life, Miss Hayes."

She came as close as she could without risking his hitting her as he went back to lifting the weights out to his sides. Not close, considering his arm-span, but close enough to make him unable to count as he raised and lowered the weights. Out of the corner of his eye he saw her cross her arms over her attention-grabbing breasts.

"I'm afraid that's not an option, Major."

The metal weights clanked as he brought them together in front of his hips. "Respecting other people's privacy is always an option."

"Not when your privacy is a matter of law—"

He jerked the weights upward. "I can't believe you called *my mother*."

"You've spoken with her?" Her tone had a sharp edge.

Boy, was she mistaken if she thought she could control Ann Branigan. No one put achieving her goals above all else like his mom.

He lowered his arms and brought the weights together. "Briefly."

"So what did you two talk about?" She sounded as though she was worried about competition for the Supreme Commander seat.

He had to admit, Lynn Hayes was the first woman he'd ever met who might actually give Ann a run for her money.

He answered, "She called me this morning to tell me she was flying down to meet with you." He tossed her a glare as he lifted his arms again. "Then she expects me to explain everything."

"Will you?"

The hope in her voice had him gritting his teeth. She still didn't get it.

"No. Why did you call her?"

"Her previous involvement with Marcus McCoy made contacting her a logical choice. I felt it was only right to inform her of his death, regardless of your level of cooperation."

"You mean 'lack thereof.'"

"Yes."

The ghost of a child's yearning for a deeper connection between the people who'd made him piggybacked on his unquestionable love for his mother and had him asking, "How'd she take the news that he'd been killed?"

"In stride."

He scoffed. "That's my mom."

"It's been a long time since she and Marcus were involved, Rick."

He ignored her soft use of his name, the way it tempted him to see her as more than another problem he *really* didn't need right now.

Aiming for a snide tone, he said, "Thirty-three years and nine months, to be exact."

She shifted in front of him and looked him in the eye. Looked deep in him again. "Ah."

He hated when she did that. "What do you mean, *ah?*"

"The whole 'Always Faithful' thing."

To hide his surprise, Rick took his time setting down the hand weights. She would make a hell of an intel officer. "What are you talking about?"

"Just something your mother mentioned."

"What my mom mentioned? About that—I don't want you talking to my mother, or anyone else I know, for that matter." He'd say the words, but he doubted she'd listen—

"Can't do that," she shot back.

He heaved a sigh, then told her flat-out, "You can and you—"

"I'm going to find out the truth about the accident, Rick." She squared her shoulders and her stance, her jaw at a belligerent angle. "I'm going to uncover the truth, then I'm going to use it to find a way to get you out of trouble and back to Dependable so the terms of your father's will can be executed. And give Joseph McCoy the gift of one of his grandsons for his seventy-fifth birthday."

He mimicked her pose, but improved on it with a squadron's worth of testosterone. "Like hell."

Chapter Four

"You should have told me the truth."

Pete Wright's pale blue eyes and battered face didn't show any sign that he was surprised by Rick's choice of greeting, or by finding the best friend of his youth on his doorstep for the first time in months. Not since Pete had left the Marines for what he swore would be greener, less "confining" pastures. He simply lifted a bony shoulder in his typical shrug. A gesture that, as Rick matured, had begun to bug the hell out of him.

Now it made him sick to his stomach.

Pete raked his long, dark brown bangs back from his face, his once-military cut gone wild. "Dude, I barely knew my own name that night, let alone the truth. I'm barbecuing out back." He turned and walked away, but left the front door to his apartment open by way of invitation. The stylized, but no less rude, gesture printed on the back of his black T-shirt sent a different message.

Rick pulled in a calming—and pretty much useless—breath and followed. The front room of the small, two-bedroom, first-floor apartment went as dark as a tomb when he closed the door behind him. The thick beige curtains were drawn over the large window to shut out the hot late-afternoon sun as well as the view of three green Dumpsters Rick had noticed in the small parking lot as he'd waited for Pete to answer the doorbell.

A stream of light knifed through the tiny eating nook when Pete elbowed his way past the same type of curtains that covered the sliding-glass doors. The screen door scraped along its metal track as he went out onto the patio.

Rick followed, clinging to his composure. He'd finally come here for the answers he hadn't wanted before. He couldn't have stopped the train once it'd started to come off the tracks and the details only would have haunted him more.

But now he had to know exactly what had happened that night, had to arm himself against the barrage of questions Lynn Hayes was sure to unleash on him.

He had to know everything, to stay one step ahead of her in her quest for the truth.

And deep down, he still held out hope that Pete would come to his senses and act honorably. He'd done it before—only at Rick's urging—but maybe he'd do it again. A stupid thing to hope for, because Rick doubted he'd be able to allow Pete to even try. They'd dug themselves in too far already, with Rick's initially taking responsibility.

The sharp smell of cooking meat along with the glare of sun on the six-by-six slab of concrete that constituted Pete's patio hit Rick when he stepped through the slider, as it had countless times before. Only this time he wasn't making a social call.

Pete was already back to manning the charcoal-briquette grill, spatula in hand. "Shut the screen door behind ya. Marissa hates flies." He pressed the spatula against one of two thick hamburger patties. "Better yet, close the slider. The heat's been getting to her. Those of us at the bottom of the hill don't have the luxury of working AC." Fat and juices sizzled and spat.

The ancient temptation to feel guilty about being among the haves when Pete had always been among the have-nots stirred in Rick's belly, but he refused to let Pete toss him on the barbie along with the burgers. Nevertheless, the pounding that had started in his head after Lynn's visit intensified to bomb blasts as he reached to close the sliding-glass door.

With heartfelt sincerity he asked, "How is Marissa?"

"As big as a house."

A feminine voice called from inside the apartment, "I heard that!"

The curtain on the other side of the sliding door Rick had been closing was moved out of the way by a very attractive, very pregnant blonde.

Rick automatically searched her warm brown eyes for any sign of accusation. "Hey, Marissa."

"Rick!" She greeted him with a wide smile softened by contentment. "Long time no see!" She pushed the patio door wide enough to hug him as best she could.

The intensity of his headache lessened as he

hugged her back. When she pulled away, he glanced at the eight months' worth of baby under her pink maternity tank top, and managed a crooked grin when he returned his gaze to hers. "I'll say. And you're growing more beautiful by the inch."

She'd been pretty, petite and trusting when Pete had first met her on the beach last summer. From what Rick could tell, only the petite part had changed, by at least forty pounds, all of it sticking out in front of her. The thought of destroying her trust made his stomach turn.

"Boy, Rick, that smile of yours is enough to flip a heart or two on a normal basis, but combined with these pregnancy hormones…" She sucked air through her teeth. "It's a good thing I'm a happily married woman."

God, he hoped so. He slid Pete a look.

Pete's attention was on the burgers.

Marissa said, "Jeez, we haven't seen you since the wedding. Can you stay for an early dinner? We've been eating our bigger meal around now so I have plenty of time to digest before I try to lie down. It'll just take me a second to make another patty—"

Rick held up a hand. "No, I can't. Sorry, Marissa. But thanks anyway."

She pouted, but she didn't seem all that disappointed. "I understand. Now that you're officially a major, you're probably as busy as all get out." She smiled brightly again. "Hey, congrats on that, by the way." She cuffed him lightly on the shoulder.

She didn't know. Rick swallowed down the bitter

taste of disappointment. He had hoped Pete would at least be honest with his wife.

Narrowing her eyes at the sun, she blew out a breath. "Holy cow, it's hot out here. Too hot for us Shamu types. If you don't mind, I'll take my whale-sized self inside and leave you guys alone to chat."

Rick glanced again at Pete, who was finally giving Rick his attention. Clearly he knew there'd be more than just chatting going on.

Pete's gaze flicked to his wife. "I can set up the umbrella for ya, babe."

Marissa wrinkled her nose. "Only if you have a block of ice for me to sit on."

Not about to let Pete hide behind his pregnant wife, Rick said, "Go on inside, Marissa. You need to stay cool."

She put a hand to her back. "What I need is to have this baby, but I'm out of luck for a good month." She smiled. "It was great seeing you, Rick. Don't be such a stranger." She gestured at the cut across her husband's nose. "Good influences seem hard to come by these days." On that ominous note she pulled the patio door closed and let the curtain drop.

Pete had begun to chip away at her trust already, after only six months of marriage.

Pressed hamburger sizzled behind Rick. "She automatically assumed I'd been in a fight, so I went with it," said Pete.

The anger and frustration that had propelled Rick down the hill from the view properties to the frayed apartment complexes returned in a rush. He wheeled on his faithless friend.

"I repeat. You should have told me the truth."

"Yeah, yeah. And I should have zigged when I zagged through that light." Pete deftly flipped one of the burgers. "It's already been established I have rotten luck."

Rick ground his back teeth together at the man's terminal resistance to taking responsibility for his actions. "Luck had nothing to do with you getting into that truck drunk and trying to drive. You chose to do it, Pete. Just as you chose to lie to me about what really happened, to get me to take the fall for you."

Pete finally faced him. "And just like I chose to save your butt in Afghanistan. You owe me, Branigan. You owe me big."

The words had never been said before, but they'd been there, hanging between them.

As if the blow had been physical, Rick's hip twinged where fragments from the hunk of shrapnel that had torn into him still resided. No way could he have gotten out alone from the tangled pile of junk his Humvee had been turned into by a hand-held rocket. He'd been so certain he was toast that day, but Pete had crawled in after him.

Now Rick was expected to do the same, even though the night of Pete's accident, Pete had simply begged for a huge favor. If he'd formally called in his marker then, Rick would have been tipped off that more was involved than a come-together with a tree and a fear of lost insurance.

It wasn't until after Rick had said yes when the police had asked if he'd been driving his truck an hour earlier, that Rick had realized what Pete was asking in exchange for having saved Rick's life.

He met Pete's pale blue eyes and cut to the chase. "My career for my life?"

Without so much as a blink, Pete shrugged. "I'd lose more than any career if I got busted for this one. Did you not notice the pregnant wife?" He leaned toward Rick and lowered his voice. "Who is only my wife because you guilted me into marrying her."

Blindsided by Pete's choice of attack, Rick stared at him. "I just told you to do the right thing. You're the one who added the guilt. And I asked you first if you loved her. Has that changed?"

Pete turned back to the grill. "Hell, no. Just the opposite." He slammed the other burger onto its uncooked side and shook his head. "That's why you gotta do this for me, man. I can't go to jail."

He looked at Rick, punctuating his words with the spatula. "With my driving record, you know that's where I'd end up for sure." He focused on the burgers again, his lean shoulders, which could never quite carry the load he'd been saddled with in life, curved forward. "Marissa can't work much longer, and her and that baby will be depending on me."

Rick's anger did some sizzling of its own. "Is that why you were at Rancho Margarita getting wasted? Because for the first time in your life you're truly responsible for more than your own good time?"

"No." Pete threw his answer at Rick along with a

glare. Then his face fell and the knee-jerk insolence melted away. "Maybe. This whole fatherhood thing scares the crap out of me."

Rick stubbornly clung to his anger. "And you're already setting such a fine example."

Pete spread his arms wide. "We've known for a long time that I'm not perfect like you, Wonder Boy." He threw the spatula onto the grill, then sighed and scrubbed a hand over his face. "Look, Rick, I'd never expect you to do this if it were just me."

Rick wasn't entirely sure he believed him.

"And you've always had enough courage for both of us. You established that loud and clear back when we were kids and my dad was knocking me around. I need you to be there for me again, man."

Rick felt a tug of the bond that had formed between them then. He tried to see past it. "This is a hell of a lot different from me sneaking into your house to get your stuff so you could stay with my mom and me for a while."

"It wouldn't have been if the old man had caught you."

"Maybe if he had, we would have been square when you pulled me out of that Humvee." But Pete's dad hadn't, and they both knew the risk Rick had taken as a thirteen-year-old was nothing compared with what Pete had done for him.

The look Pete gave him clearly said, *Yeah, but he didn't, so we're not.* He pointed toward town. "Any decent lawyer can get you a deal with the prosecutor. You've never made a mistake in your life. The

D.A. isn't going to hang you out to dry on your first offense."

"The Marines don't care if it's my first or not. It'll be seen as a breach of the code of conduct."

"So you'll get a letter of reprimand in your file." Pete waved away the importance of a besmirched record. "Welcome to the club."

Frustration burned a hole in Rick's sternum. Pete really didn't have a clue what was important to Rick.

Pete stepped close, the "Hey, what's the big stink?" look gone from his angular face, replaced by a desperate fierceness Rick had never seen. "If you won't do it for me, do it for Marissa. Do it for our baby."

The smell of burning meat mingled with the acrid taste of obligation in the back of Rick's throat. Where did a man draw the line with *Semper Fi?* How could he possibly be always faithful to everyone?

His head pounded.

He couldn't.

As much as he loved the Marines, he wouldn't doom an innocent baby to a rougher start in life than it already had coming.

Rick laughed bitterly at his own rationalizations. All the possible outs, all the reasons for acting on them or not, were moot. He'd already claimed responsibility.

Now he had to follow through, whatever the outcome.

Gesturing toward the smoking grill, Rick said flatly, "You need to rescue Marissa's dinner. And while you're doing it, tell me everything you can remember about the night of the accident."

Rick needed to know everything so he could devise a plan to thwart the McCoys' beautiful lawyer and take the fall on *his* terms.

Honorably.

OUTSIDE THE STRIP-MALL office of Acme Legal Services, Lynn dropped her head back against the headrest of her rental car, waiting for the blasting air-conditioning to cool the car's interior. Only time could cool her irritation with the lawyer Rick had hired.

Rick.

She raised her head just enough to *thunk* it back against the padded headrest. She'd just thought of the major by his given name. She'd only used it during her last conversation with him in a vain attempt to get him to see reason, but thinking of him that way had apparently sunk roots. On a personal level.

Wonderful. Almost as wonderful as the apathy his lawyer had just exhibited during her brief visit with him. Not even hints of substantial monetary gratitude from her wealthy, influential employer—whom she of course couldn't name—could get the whopping two partners who happened to make up the entire firm of Acme Legal to give a damn about the Branigan case.

How could they not jump at a chance to improve their circumstances? What kind of lawyers were they, for crying out loud?

She wanted this case to be as quick and easy as they did, but they weren't remotely willing to pressure Rick to plead guilty to a lesser charge, let alone look into the circumstances surrounding the arrest. After being chewed out for the initial plea of not guilty at arraignment, the one handling Rick's case had done what the client had asked of him, nothing more, nothing less. He hadn't checked out anything, and had no more information than she had.

To them Rick was just another jarhead insisting on using the rights he might one day have to give his life for. They didn't care why he might be refusing to tell his side of the story, taking his right to remain silent to the maximum. Talk about one big, frustrating dead end.

So it would be up to her to interview the witnesses, the people who'd served Branigan at the bar, the arresting officers, the woman in the other car and Branigan's friends.

As quickly as possible.

Time was not her ally.

She might as well start at the beginning. She raised her head and put her car into gear to drive to the bar where Rick had supposedly gotten drunk. She'd use the directions she'd copied from the Internet.

Oceanedge turned out to be a thriving blend of thousands of military families and people who simply wanted to live near the Pacific Ocean. Not to mention a ton of tourists. A far cry from quiet Dependable, Missouri.

As she traveled west on MacArthur Boulevard, squinting into the sun despite wearing her sunglasses, she gave up on the air conditioner and rolled down her window. The crisp ocean breeze carried the scent of salt and what would be for some a spirit-reviving freshness.

She just wanted to be cooled off. Though sleeveless, the cream satin shell under her suit coat was sticking to her.

Everything was sticking to her. She needed answers. She had to gather enough information to find a way out of this in a day or two. Three, tops. She had to. And she *would not* let what she discovered matter to her.

Innocent or guilty, Rick Branigan was simply a means to an end. The next step up in her career. If she stayed on track, there was no limit to what she could achieve.

Slowly feeling more like her old self—confident and assured—Lynn turned onto the street that led to the first stop in her investigation.

The bar looked exactly as she'd imagined a bar near a huge military base would. Prosperous. The large, cream stucco building, topped by a red tile roof, stood alone on a bluff with a view of the Pacific out the back. A green neon sign shaped like a margarita glass in one of the tinted windows proclaimed the Rancho Margarita. The acres of asphalt parking were almost full and she had to search for a space.

Shoot. She'd been hoping it was early enough that the waitstaff would be free to give her their full attention when she talked to them. Early enough that the smells, the noise, the "good-time" atmosphere wouldn't stir memories she would prefer to remain stagnant.

Undaunted, she grabbed her briefcase, climbed out of her rental car and headed for the big barnlike

front door. The dark metal handle had been fash-
ioned to look like a margarita-glass-shaped branding
iron.

Inside, she paused long enough to take off her sunglasses and slip Rick's mug shot from her briefcase
before glancing around the place. The interior of Rancho Margarita, decorated much like the exterior, was
brighter than she'd expected thanks to the wall of
windows facing the ocean, but heavily tinted glass
muted most of the direct early-evening sunlight. Still,
the place was a long way from a Louisiana dive.

The place also had a lot more tables than the typical bar, all arranged around the central bar where the
drinks were made. Two white-shirt-clad men worked
within the space between the dark wood bar and an is-
land of liquor bottles. All shapes of glasses hung from
racks above their heads. Clearly, you could get more
than just margaritas at Rancho Margarita. Patrons
could also play pool in a separate area off to the side.

At the moment, everyone was mostly eating and
laughing loudly over the Jimmy Buffett music piped
throughout the place. Not exactly ranch music, but
it sure fit with the drinks being served.

Lynn tuned it all out and headed for the bar. Both
bartenders glanced up as she came toward them, but
the older one waved the other away, with an air of
being very much in charge. She went straight for
him. A big, square man from his buzzed graying hair
to his beefy hands, he seemed ready for battle as he
set aside the martini shaker he'd been wiping.

She realized too late that maybe the power suit,

pastel blue or not, hadn't been her best wardrobe choice for this visit. Corporate America put some people on the defensive. She was here on business, however, so she might as well look it—though she knew enough about men to pause and free her hair from the bun she'd twisted it into; a little distracting femininity could go a long way.

"What can I do for you, ma'am?" His hard-edged voice matched the rest of him. Probably a retired drill sergeant or something, especially with the "ma'am" thing, which she was beginning to find annoying despite its respectfulness.

She held up the photo of Rick appearing every inch the stubborn Marine, an expression she was starting to think of as his self-defense mode. "Have you seen this man in here?"

"Yep."

Her heart took a little dip, and it had nothing to do with her instincts being proven wrong. Why she'd want Rick to really be all honor and trustworthiness was beyond her.

"When?"

"Right now." The bartender pointed over her shoulder.

From behind her, a familiar deep voice that held a dangerous persuasiveness asked, "Can I buy you a drink?"

She whirled to face USMC Major Rick Branigan. This time her heart started to pound.

"You shouldn't be here," she hissed.

"A guy's gotta eat."

"Not in a bar when he's out on bail for DUI vehicular assault. How long have you been here?"

"The law insists I'm innocent until proven guilty, ma'am." He neatly sidestepped her question.

She wanted to grind her teeth. "Easily done when there's no defense *offered*. And stop calling me ma'am. I'm not that old."

"No, you most certainly aren't. But respect should be given where respect is due."

"Oh, please. I'm also not that dumb. You can't tell me to get lost one day, then claim to respect me the next."

He tucked a hand in his jeans pocket. "I most certainly can. And I wouldn't have respected you if you'd done as I'd told you and gotten lost. It's the fact that you haven't that has earned my respect."

She narrowed her eyes, searching for the backhand in his convoluted compliment, or, more likely, the ulterior motive. "I won't be lulled into believing you're no longer hostile to my involvement."

"Can't say that lulling was on my agenda today, Lynn."

She started at his use of her name, not liking one bit the little riot of whatever it was he'd touched off in her stomach. She pointed a finger at him. "Now you're trying to manipulate me. Somehow."

"Somehow?"

"You used my name."

He spread an arm wide. "You said I couldn't call you ma'am, and it doesn't seem right to sit with you here in this bar and call you Miss Hayes the whole time."

His Mr. Friendly routine convinced her he was up to something. Most likely tampering with a witness. She had no way of knowing if he'd arrived before or after her.

She gestured to the bartender, who was watching their exchange with interest. "You can't have any interaction with the people who served you that night."

"The only person I want to interact with here is you." He jerked a thumb toward one of the few open tables. "Let's sit down. I hear they have great chicken sandwiches."

Her pulse leaped at his possible slip. "You *hear* they have great chicken sandwiches?"

He reached past her to grab a handful of peanuts from a small basket on the bar and popped some in his mouth. "I've only had the salted nuts."

Her stomach lurched. What had happened to not letting what she found out matter?

He curled his hand around her elbow to lead her away. She could feel his fingers through her jacket. Tingles shot up her arm.

She pulled her elbow from his grasp. "I need to talk to the bartender."

He shrugged and walked to a nearby table and sat, then gestured to the men behind the bar. "Those two weren't working that night."

She crossed her arms. "Forgive me for not being willing to take your word for it. If you don't mind, I'll ask for myself."

He swept a hand indulgently toward the bar.

"Wouldn't expect anything different from a woman like you."

"A woman like me?" She echoed the feminine variation of the question he'd asked her yesterday.

"The ambitious, do-it-herself type. Grew up with one, in case you didn't notice during your breakfast meeting this morning."

Jeez, he did a number on her insides. She suddenly felt more than a little ill.

Rick *did* think she was like his mother. Which meant he'd be inclined to do the opposite of what she wanted.

Bad. Very bad.

Only, she knew that she was driven not by ambition, but by gut-munching fear.

Chapter Five

Lawyer Lady commenced storming the bar, briefcase in hand and beautiful black hair tumbling down her back in soft waves, moving in time with a few of her other waves.

Rick pulled his wayward attention from her curvy backside and met the gaze of retired Gunnery Sergeant Benjamin Kloppman who stood on guard behind the bar. A slight shake of the head was all it took to convey to Gunny that Rick didn't want him to cooperate with Miss Hayes's questioning.

Rick certainly didn't look forward to the grilling Gunny would give him later. He'd just have to convince Gunny—and the other friends whose help he'd need—to trust him. While he couldn't count on them to agree with what he was doing, he could count on them to help him if he asked them to.

Once she reached the bar, the striking woman repeatedly pointed in Rick's direction and Gunny repeatedly shrugged. Fortunately, he probably didn't have to lie. Rick seriously doubted Gunny had been working the night Pete had tied one on. Gunny would never have let Pete walk out with car keys in hand.

Gunny would just have to feign confusion about who had been behind the bar that night and somehow fend off any request to speak with someone who did know.

Lynn's gestures became more animated, her composure clearly slipping. She probably figured the last people able to best her were a bunch of ground grunts. But infantrymen stuck together.

She pulled a file out of her briefcase and flipped it open with the smoothness of a marksman shouldering his weapon. The woman definitely had style.

And according to his lawyer, who'd called him the second she'd left his office, she also played by her own rules. She'd been willing to do anything, even offer a blatant bribe, to get Acme Legal Services to ignore its client's wishes in favor of her and the McCoys' agenda. Thank goodness his lawyer had already walked away from that sort of corporate greed once before and hadn't been tempted a second time.

Having failed to draft his lawyer onto her team or milk any additional information from him or his partner, Miss Hayes had of course headed to the starting point of that fateful night—this bar—in an attempt to find out the truth. Which Rick couldn't let her do.

He'd had to put off his mother, who'd wanted to see him, and scramble to get here just moments before Lynn arrived. He'd been lucky thus far. From now on, though, he would have no choice but to stick to her as best he could to sabotage her investigative efforts. Not to mention call in more than a few favors to keep her from learning anything of importance.

Namely, his connection with Pete Wright, whom everyone knew was destined to get it wrong.

Miss Hayes pushed her glossy black hair back from her face in irritation and Rick realized he'd been staring at the tumbled mass. He'd nearly swallowed his tongue when she'd removed a single long hairpin from her bun and all that thick, shining hair had fallen free.

He'd figured her hair would be long, but he'd had no idea how much it would add to her already stunning appearance.

With one knee cocked and the toe of a pointy tan high heel tapping furiously, she remained focused for a moment on the papers within the file. Then she gestured at one of the cocktail waitresses sporting Rancho Margarita logo T-shirts, short denim skirts beneath their white aprons and cowboy boots.

Gunny shrugged.

She pointed at the other.

Another shrug.

The file snapped closed. Man, steam should be whistling out of her pretty ears at any second.

Instead, she offered a gracious nod, picked up her briefcase and walked back to his table. Rick made a mental note never to play poker with her; her current expression revealed nothing of the agitation her body had been broadcasting a moment ago.

Not surprisingly, the thought of her body and all that midnight hair brought to mind strip poker. Under different circumstances, the rewards definitely would have been worth the challenge of discovering her "tells" that would reveal if she was bluffing or holding a winning hand.

As she set her briefcase in the chair across from him, the left corner of her full, rose-tinted mouth ticked downward, and there was no mistaking the tightness in her shoulders. Apparently, discovering her "tells" wouldn't be that challenging after all. Maybe he could shake her resolve to discover the truth sooner than he had thought.

He stood and pulled out a chair next to the one he'd occupied. She accepted the offered seat without looking at him, but her exotic scent washed over him and woke the troops. Maybe she'd be shaking *his* resolve to keep her at a distance soon.

He brushed off the threat. Nothing could convince him to choose self-preservation over doing the honorable thing.

Nothing could make him the same as the man who had fathered him.

Rick sat down again and studied the woman bent on complicating an already difficult situation. She still hadn't looked at him, intent on straightening her pastel blue suit jacket with a controlled casualness he realized was another "tell." She clearly didn't like not getting her way but was fighting hard not to let it show. She'd be a good leader.

And she really was gorgeous. He already knew from seeing her in the harsh sunlight that she had flawless skin, but in the bar's soft light her complexion glowed. Especially with the jet-black hair framing her finely-boned face. She'd relaxed her lips slightly, and he was struck by how kissable they looked.

His primed body agreed wholeheartedly, and blood started heading south. As if invited along for the ride, his attention drifted down to her neckline and the shadow of her cleavage. Very kissable, too.

Physical attraction to her was the last thing he needed. He shifted in his chair and jerked his gaze from her mouth to her eyes.

She was watching him. And judging by the stunned expression in her wide amber eyes, had figured out exactly what he'd been thinking. So much for playing poker with her.

Because there was no defense for what he'd been doing, he went on offense. "What?"

The surprise faded, replaced by a slightly disgruntled and far-too-jaded amusement. She lifted one corner of her tempting mouth. "I didn't think you were the ogling sort."

He grinned at her acknowledgment of the discoveries they'd made about each other yesterday. For whatever stupid-assed reason, she had truly ceased to be Miss Hayes to him.

"Sorry to disappoint, Lynn."

She fought a wider smile, clearly not going to let him off the hook for messing up her investigation that easily. "Then we definitely need to find you something else to do." She heaved a dramatic sigh. "Because I doubt you'd be willing to give straightforward answers to my questions, how about we order a couple of those sandwiches you mentioned."

The tension in his neck relaxed a little. "That's what I'm here for."

She actually snorted. "I bet." Still, she raised a hand to catch the attention of one of the waitresses. When the young, bouncy blonde reached their table and smiled a greeting, Lynn glanced between him and the waitress, her hawklike eyes searching for some sign of recognition from either of them.

She wasn't going to get one.

Pencil poised, the waitress asked, "What can I get you two?"

Before he could open his mouth, Lynn said, "By any chance were you here the night of June—"

"Two chicken sandwiches, please. The works."

Though the waitress scribbled down the order and continued to smile, she raised her brows at him for so blatantly interrupting his companion. "Fries?"

He nodded. "Definitely."

He caught Lynn's brief and pointed glare out of the corner of one eye. When she returned her attention to the waitress, undoubtedly to try again, he added, "And two of your house-special margaritas."

The waitress nodded and produced two drink napkins sporting the bar's margarita-glass logo from her apron pocket. "Can do." She placed the napkins in front of Lynn. "Anything else—"

"Kim?" Gunny called, saving the day. When the waitress turned toward him, he gestured her over to the bar in a way that would make anyone hop-to.

She was already moving as she told them, "I'll get your order right in."

Lynn raised a hand. "Wait—"

But Kim was on her way without a backward glance.

Rick and Lynn both watched as she hurried to the bar and leaned close so Gunny could murmur something to her. Rick could tell she wanted to look back at their table, but she didn't. She simply nodded, then said something back, probably giving him their drink order, before walking briskly toward the kitchen, on the other side of the bar.

Lynn made a noise low in her throat as she returned her attention to him. "Nice. Very nice."

"Oh, good. Some women don't go for men ordering for them."

"What I don't *go for* is men who keep me from doing my job." So she clearly wasn't amused.

"You don't have a job here, Lynn, so why don't we just enjoy ourselves."

"Woo-hoo," she said with zero enthusiasm.

As if on cue, the lights in the bar dimmed further to create a dinner ambience, even though it was still relatively early in the evening.

He looked up at the green glass light-fixture hanging over their table. "Ah. Mood lighting."

Obviously unimpressed, she crossed her arms on the table and leaned toward him. "So, let me guess. The bartender is a buddy of yours."

He did the same. "So, let me guess. You were just pretending to give up so you could get a shot at questioning one of the waitresses."

"Bingo. Who's the bartender? An ex-Marine, right?"

"There are no ex-Marines, only former Marines."

"My mistake. Who is he?"

"Retired Gunnery Sergeant Benjamin Kloppman."

"Kloppman?"

She was probably filing the name away in her mental Rolodex. He'd have to make sure Gunny's helping didn't cost him.

"Gunny. All gunnery sergeants are called Gunny, even after they retire."

"Must make for a lot of confusion at the Christmas party," she quipped, and reached out to twirl her drink napkin.

Rick chuckled, liking how she dealt with her frustration.

Kim returned with their drinks, nearly sloshing them on the table in her haste. "Here you go! Two house-special margaritas. Enjoy!" Then she was off again. She'd kept talking so Lynn wouldn't have a chance to get a word in edgewise. He owed Gunny double.

Lynn just sat there with her mouth slightly open for a moment, then snapped it shut and picked up what seemed to be a run-of-the-mill lime margarita on the rocks. "Might as well *enjoy*."

"Atta girl." He toasted her and they both took a drink. "Umm. Better than I thought."

"So you weren't drinking the house special the night of the accident?"

He blew out a breath. "No. I was not." He hadn't

cracked his first of two beers until after Pete had brought the truck back.

"That's right. The arresting officer noted you were drinking beer," she mused. "How many was it again?"

"Do you play pool?"

"No." Her answer came fast and clipped.

"Really? I wouldn't have thought there'd be anything you'd admit to not being able to do."

"Why's that?"

"Because you're the can-do sort."

In unison they said, "Sorry to disappoint."

Rick laughed and shook his head. "Seems we have a theme going here."

"Apparently."

He sat back in his chair and threw up his hands. "Okay, enough's enough. No more preconceived notions about each other."

She studiously repositioned her drink on its napkin. "I threw mine out already."

Rick slowly lowered his hands. He shouldn't ask. He shouldn't. But his curiosity—okay, make that ego—over what a woman like her thought of him, won out over his good sense. Maybe he'd been a little too focused on his career a little too long.

He crossed his arms over his chest. "Why's that?"

"Because nothing jibes, Rick. Nothing adds up. Even if you were a personality of extremes, giving all to your career but cutting loose and partying just as hard, there are still too many inconsistencies. Too many red flags. Something's going on with you, and the only way I can deal with it and do my job is to figure out what that something is."

"And I've already made it clear I don't want you to."

"I know," she said softly, as if his answer was all the confirmation she needed that ignoring his wishes was the right thing to do. "But I can't stand by and let an innocent person take the rap."

"I thought corporate lawyers weren't supposed to care about guilt or innocence."

"In this case it's starting to matter to me. A personal weakness I'm normally not troubled by."

The reluctant admission touched something deep in his chest. He was always the one riding to the rescue, doing the championing. When was the last time anyone had championed him?

He uncrossed his arms and stared into her glowing amber eyes, recognizing that while she might not have the power to shake his resolve to take the fall for Pete, she had the power to make him care about her.

Holy crap.

Kim burst into the emotionally charged air surrounding their table to deliver the chicken sandwiches with the same flurry and chatter she'd used when delivering their drinks.

Lynn blinked quickly and sat back from the table, a rising flush visible in her cheeks even in the low light.

An unspoken truce was called as they ate, but he couldn't keep from watching her. Her concentration stayed firmly on her food, which she was eating but didn't seem to be enjoying.

He remembered how she'd marched into his

condo with her three goals. Two had to do with what the McCoys wanted—getting him to Dependable without fuss in time for Joseph McCoy's seventy-fifth birthday party. The third she'd said was personal. Which of those goals would she be jeopardizing the most by looking for the truth?

If he could figure that out, he might be able to stop her.

She'd barely made it through half of her chicken sandwich in the time it took him to polish off his. He wiped his mouth with his paper napkin and rested his elbows on the table. "Are you originally from Missouri, Lynn?"

She flinched, dribbling a drop of mayonnaise onto her chin. "Um—" she used a knuckle to wipe off her chin while she finished chewing "—Louisiana, actually."

"That explains the hint of sultry Southern accent."

She choked and had to grab for her drink to wash the bite all the way down.

Surprised at himself for opening his mouth without thinking, he waved off the comment. "Where in Louisiana?" Realizing she had a French look about her, he guessed. "New Orleans?"

"I was born there, yes."

"But that's not where you grew up?"

She put her sandwich down on her plate. "Not entirely."

He waited for her to elaborate, but she simply picked up a fry and dabbed it in the mayonnaise that had escaped her sandwich.

"Did you grow up in Missouri?"

"No."

Beginning to feel that he was the lawyer and she was the uncooperative client, he tried again. "Have you lived long in Dependable?"

She shrugged. "A while."

Clearly, she didn't want to play "so, tell me about yourself." Finding out her "personal goal" could be tougher than he thought.

To help things along, he offered, "I'm wholly a product of the San Francisco Bay area."

A corner of her mouth inched upward. "Yes, I know."

"Of course you do. Which puts us on unequal footing. What about your parents? They still live in Louisiana? How about siblings? Half or otherwise?"

She dropped the French fry on her plate and met his gaze. "How about that game of pool?"

She was back in poker mode, her eyes revealing as much as she was apparently willing to reveal about herself, which was nothing. Being so shuttered must be a prerequisite for the high-priced lawyer set.

He gestured to her mostly full plate. "Don't you want to finish your sandwich?"

"No. I'm done." As if to prove it, she pushed the plate toward the center of the table.

"Okay. I'll teach you how to play." He stood and helped her with her chair, then allowed her to lead the way to the three pool tables occupying a room off to the side.

No one was playing, so they had their pick. Lynn

headed straight for the front table. Probably to make it easier for her to snag one of the other waitresses for a quick question or two.

Rick caught her elbow lightly, trying to ignore her scent and the urge to grab her elsewhere. "Let's play on the back one. It has better felt."

She gave him an assessing look, because the Kelly green felt covering each table appeared to have exactly the same amount of wear. "If you say so."

"I do."

"This being your favorite hangout and all."

He simply grunted at her relentless trolling for tidbits pertaining to his case, then guided her to a rack of pool cues on the back wall and selected one for each of them. He was by no means an expert, but he had played enough through the years with his fellow Marines to be able to show her the ropes.

"Here." He handed her a cue stick, tip up, and picked up a blue chalk cube from the tray on the bottom of the rack. "Hold the cue steady and I'll chalk you up."

"To experience?"

He shifted his attention to her. While her eyes were still shuttered, that one corner of her mouth had twitched upward.

Damn, he liked it when she joked. "Most definitely." He rubbed the indented side of the cube over her cue's tip. "But also so that you can strike the cue ball better."

She eyed the blue chalk on the end of her stick. "Doesn't it give you blue balls?"

"Oh, you're funny." But she was, and he wished he could say that he didn't enjoy her company when she wasn't trying to mess up his already messed-up world.

She grimaced, wrinkling her nose in a way that made her look younger and playful. "Sorry. Bad habit."

"Being funny?"

"Being a smart-aleck." She lightly blew the excess chalk off the cue stick.

Her self-deprecation made him soften his tone. "Beats the hell out of rantin' and ravin' when you're stressed and frustrated."

Her gaze jumped to his, revealing for a moment that he'd startled her with an accurate assessment. Then she smiled. "The night's still young, Major."

Before he could do more than match her smile, she turned away to face the pool table.

"Now, dazzle me with your skill."

He suppressed the urge to salute. "Yes, ma'am. How much do you know?"

"The rudiments."

"Good enough."

The table was set up and ready for play, with the multicolored balls racked into the starting triangle and the white cue ball at the opposite end.

Rick went to that side of the table and bent to aim his pool stick at the white ball. "I'll break to get us started."

"Very kind of you."

He glanced at her, but she was watching the table, waiting for him to scatter the balls and determine which ones they'd each be playing.

Returning his attention to what he was doing—as much as he could with her near—he ran the stick back and forth beneath his crooked left index finger to be certain of his aim, then struck the cue ball hard and sent it crashing into the other balls.

One of the white balls with a single, wide, colored stripe ricocheted into the far right pocket and a solid-colored ball clattered into a side pocket.

Rick straightened. "I guess I'll call stripes. You can be solids. We won't bother calling our shots."

She nodded and moved toward where the cue ball was coming to a stop. "You did that very well."

He scoffed. "If I'd done it well, I would have sunk two or more of the same type."

"But at least you didn't bury the cue."

Suspicion stirred in his belly at her easy use of pool lingo. He narrowed his eyes at her. "No, I didn't."

She stopped in the process of taking what had looked to be a very competent stance despite her constricting suit coat. She blinked, then raised her brows. "Is this right?"

"Yes."

She frowned and moved the elbow of the arm holding the thicker end of the stick. "Are you sure? It doesn't feel right." She took her shot anyway. The cue ball glanced off the wrong side of the seven ball and screamed straight into the opposite corner pocket.

"Maybe you should take off your jacket."

Lynn set her stick against the table and started

yanking her jacket off. "You know, it *is* kind of hot in here."

And getting hotter now that he had an eyeful of what she'd hidden beneath her jacket. The sleeveless, silky top with a softly rolled V neckline exposed her toned arms and clung to her full breasts and slender back like the best lingerie.

Speaking of lingerie, her lacy bra was faintly visible through the thin material of her top.

Something he shouldn't be noticing.

Just as he shouldn't care that both of them were obviously feeling the heat.

She tossed her jacket over a chair against the wall and pulled in a deep, breast-lifting breath before she looked at him.

Awareness was definitely there, but he couldn't read in her face what effect it was having on her. No "tells" this time.

He hoped he was being as successful at hiding what she was doing to him.

He grabbed the cue ball out of the tray the pockets funneled into and smacked it down behind the diamond markings along the edge of his end of the table. He didn't bother to line it up for any shot in particular. He hit it hard, but the clatter of pool balls coming together was no match for the pounding of blood in his ears. Since when did he have trouble controlling himself?

Since his life had stopped being his own.

Chapter Six

No.

Twisting the cue stick in his grip, Rick rejected the idea of being completely helpless to his fate. He *was* still in control.

Lynn wasn't talking to anyone who might have been working the night Pete got drunk here. She wasn't getting the answers she had declared she'd get.

Rick simply needed to keep it that way.

"Didn't any of yours go in?"

Her question brought him back to the moment. Damn, he hadn't noticed if he'd sunk any of the striped pool balls. Okay, so there was control, and then there was *control.*

"No," he guessed. Lynn was watching him—and obviously not the table—too closely for him to peek at the ball tray.

"Then I suppose I'm up." She smoothed her hands down her light blue pants and retrieved her stick, displaying a lot more poise than she'd set it down with. She was clearly not about to relinquish her control, either.

Moving around the table to where the white ball had come to rest near the corner next to him after re-bounding off the opposite end, she commented, "You play pool very forcefully, Rick."

She lined up behind the cue ball and bent slowly over the table, flipping her long black hair to one side.

Cream silk pulled, blue pants stretched, and the snarky rejoinder about Marines and their skills died in his throat.

Her softly rounded hips shifted and her back arched subtly. "Do you play here often, Rick?" She ran the pool stick back and forth beneath her crooked finger very slowly.

"Uh…" Was it his imagination, or was she taking more time aiming than she needed?

She hit the ball too low, and it practically skipped across the table, missing everything. At least she didn't launch the thing.

"Oh, darn." She slowly straightened back up.

Oh, darn? He'd agreed to knock off with the pre-conceived notions, but no way was she the "oh, darn" type. It dawned on him that she was using her sexuality and his awareness of it to distract him enough that he might slip up with his answers.

He brought his back teeth together with a *click*. Two could play at that game.

He sauntered to the end of the table, his eyes never leaving her. "I'd sure as hell play here often if the scenery was always this good."

She cocked her head at him, and some of her hair spilled off the slick silk covering her breast. "What does the scenery usually look like, then? Another *former* Marine friend?"

"I have all sorts of friends." He bent to hit the cue ball, intending to kiss it off the side, then back toward a ball in front of a side pocket.

She bowed down into his line of vision, her cleavage dead ahead. "Like who?"

He took his shot. Just because he knew her current battle plan didn't equal being immune to it. At least he hit the cue ball. Barely. It limped to a stop right up against the ball he'd meant to knock into the side pocket.

He muttered something a lot more satisfying than "oh, darn."

She was still waiting for his answer, which he wasn't going to give, so as he straightened he said, "Boy, I didn't leave you with much of a shot. Impossible, actually."

"I'll manage."

The cue ball was closest to her side of the table, but she walked around it, as if considering her options.

Rick saw the maneuver coming. Still, when she squeezed between him and the table, putting blue slacks in contact with denim, his breath caught.

But he didn't step back. He placed a hand on her waist as though she needed steadying, and felt the heat of her skin, amplified through her silk top. She *had* needed to take off her jacket. Good. He shouldn't have to be the only one to sweat this out.

When she moved past him, he trailed his hand along the rise of her hipbone. "Got it figured out yet?"

"Working on it."

He had a feeling she meant more than just her next shot.

She started to address the cue ball from the side, but raised her stick, changing her mind. "So?"

He followed after her. "So, what?"

"Who do you normally play pool here with?"

"I thought we were playing pool, not twenty questions."

"I tend to multitask." Throwing out a curvy hip, she dropped the butt of her stick onto the floor and leaned her weight on it. "Tell you what. How about we play for questions."

"Play for questions?"

"Yes." She gestured at the table. "For every ball I sink, you have to answer a question." She leveled a finger at him. "Truthfully and coherently. No, make that *honorably*."

"The same for you, right?"

She had a killer suspicious look. Eyes narrowed slightly, sharp and probing. Her chin lowered, accenting the downward cant of her brows. "Regarding what?"

"When I sink a shot. You have to answer my questions. *Honorably*. Assuming there is such a thing among corporate lawyers."

She snorted.

Rick wasn't sure if it was in amusement or agreement.

With a short nod she said, "Deal." She hoisted her stick and completely changed the way she approached the shot. She even changed the way she held the pool stick, loosening her grip, her motions more fluid.

His battle instincts kicked in.

Sure enough, she drew the stick back only once and hit the cue ball dead-on, sinking one of her balls in the corner pocket without so much as nicking his. The cue ball rolled gently back to her, and stopped in perfect position for her next shot. It'd been an impossible shot and she'd made it like a pro.

Rick frowned fiercely. "Hey…"

Brows innocently raised, she shrugged as she straightened. "Lucky shot?"

The pool stick in the crook of his elbow, he crossed his arms over his chest. "Let me guess, you're a pool shark, too."

"Not at all." She resumed her sexy hip-out position. "Okay, then. Let's cut through the baloney. You weren't the one driving—"

Rick dove for cover. "I normally play pool with other Marines. Current and former."

"That's not the question I asked you this time, Major."

"But it's the question I'm answering."

A tendril of long black hair swayed as she shook her head. "No, no. You agreed—"

He stepped close to her and spoke low. "You failed to specify which question I had to answer, Counselor. Stating only that I had to answer *a* question."

Her lip twitched as if she'd love to snarl at him. "And people wonder why contracts are so onerous."

He smiled down into her eyes, openly acknowledging her frustration and his admiration for how she handled things not going her way.

The look of frustration faded and she smiled back. "But I also have another shot."

Needing a defensive maneuver, and quick, he came up behind her. "Here, let me help you set up for it."

Over her shoulder she said, "You know, I think I have a handle on this game. But thanks, anyway."

"I insist. It'd be the *honorable* thing not to let you rely on luck twice in a row."

Before she could answer, he reached around her. There was nothing impersonal about the way he touched her.

Her breath quickened when he bent her forward over the table, and there was absolutely nothing honorable about the thoughts charging through his mind. She fit so well against him. But he couldn't let himself forget she was against him in more ways than physically.

With his mouth close to her ear, he murmured, "I'd go for the number five ball, far pocket." He lined her up whether she wanted him to or not, but because he *was* honorable, he let go of the stick and allowed her to make the shot.

The five ball rattled off the entrance to the far pocket. It didn't go in.

She made the growling noise that was becoming as familiar as her humor, and her body slumped beneath him. She was so singular in her purpose, every inch of her clearly committed to her goal.

He wondered if she allowed it to isolate her as it had his mother.

"Who are your friends, Lynn?"

"Friends get in the way."

Taken aback by her dark answer and even darker tone, he asked, "Of what?"

She froze. "Uh…"

A little too much honesty, maybe? A slip after losing her upper hand?

He eased her up. "Of work? Of what you want to achieve? Like that third goal of yours?"

Breathing deeply, she dipped out of his arms, and he let her go. Though she kept her face averted, he could see a red flush on the fair skin of her slender neck and jaw. After she'd put some distance between them, she turned to face him. Her eyes were bright, the amber glowing with anger.

Definitely a slip.

She jerked her head toward the table. "You haven't sunk a ball yet."

"You're right. I haven't." He surveyed the table. Fortunately, her failed attempt to send home the number five solid had left him with an easy shot at two stripes lined up in front of the other corner pocket. A quick look at her confirmed she knew it, too.

Rick drove the cue ball hard into them and planted both balls. He straightened and leaned on his stick. "There. One to earn the question I've already asked and had answered, and the second for the other question. What do friends get in the way of?"

She raised her chin, and he thought for sure she wasn't going to answer.

Then she surprised him by stating, "No ties, no limits."

"Come again?"

"No ties, no limits. If I don't have any ties to anyone, I can't be limited. There will be nothing standing in my way of achieving the kind of security that doesn't go away. That can't be stripped away." She threw out an arm. "Satisfied?"

He'd recognized there was more to her than he'd thought, but he'd had no idea just how much. The strength that he already admired stemmed from something unexpected, something dark. And he was stupid for wanting to find out more.

Especially because he suspected he wanted to find out more for reasons other than to stop her from meddling. The plain fact was, she intrigued him.

Every instinct he possessed screamed, *Incoming!*

She waved a hand at the table. "Go ahead with your next shot. You're bound to miss sometime, then it will be *my* turn. And I guarantee you, I won't miss again."

"How can you be so sure?"

"You have to earn that answer."

He moved around to the end of the table and did just that, sending a ball home with a clatter.

She paid up without preamble. "Because it's amazing what you can learn when you're ten years old, sitting in the corner of a bar's poolroom, waiting for your parents' luck to run out so you can go home."

LYNN BLINKED TWICE before the magnitude of what she'd said sank in, releasing a flood of ice-cold horror that froze the blood in her veins. The heat that had been stinging her cheeks, throat and chest drained away, carrying with it the haze that had clouded her thinking.

Never in her life had she revealed such a thing, under any circumstance, let alone to a man so closely linked to what she was after. From her teens on, she'd done everything she could to distance herself from that part of her life, in the choices she made all the way down to how she talked. She didn't want any reminders of that lost little girl she'd been, at the mercy of her irresponsible parents. Her life was going to be as different as possible. It had to be.

Unwilling to be vulnerable to anyone, she'd worked hard at living by her motto of "no ties, no limits."

Clearly, he also had the power to unsettle her in a way no one had ever done.

He might think she had a sultry Southern accent, but he had the McCoy sexuality in spades. Normally something she wouldn't have any trouble with; she was not easily impressed. But there was something about Rick that had thrown her off from their first meeting.

Was it his unexpected reaction to her presence here? She shouldn't have to be fighting him for his freedom.

And he wasn't saying anything. He simply stared at her with those blue eyes, certainly debating whether or not to comment on the elephant she'd tossed out between them.

She couldn't breathe. How stupid, *stupid* of her to lose her cool like that.

She needed out of there. Needed to put distance between them.

It wasn't as though she'd be changing his mind or getting crucial information—or any information at all—out of him, so keeping away from him would be the best thing right now. She'd revealed way, way too much about herself to be effective anymore. She'd have to stick with her plan of finding out the truth from other sources.

And though she'd risk exposing him to the threat of the sort of publicity Joseph McCoy wanted to avoid, she could go to these "former and current" Marine friends of his behind his back and get them to convince him to cooperate. A call to Joseph himself—heaven help her—was also in order.

Because Rick's ability to penetrate her armor was freaking her out.

"Lynn!"

She jerked, and realized he'd taken a step toward her.

"I said, I'm sorry."

Making her movements deliberate so she didn't visibly shake, she placed the pool stick on the table. "Not your problem."

"Doesn't keep me from being sorry."

Those blue eyes seemed to access a part of her no one had seen for a very, very long time. He took another step closer.

Distance. She eased back.

He stopped, and something passed across his handsome face. Something that smacked of understanding. Or more likely, pity.

Spotting her jacket where she'd dumped it on a nearby chair, she used retrieving it as an excuse to dodge away from him. "Yes, well. As much as I've enjoyed myself, this has been a wholly unproductive day, and I don't envision it improving." Not as long as he was around, at least. Her sole hope was to go where he wasn't.

And there was only one place she could be guaranteed of that.

Renewed determination brought her chin up.

"Lynn—"

"You'll be contacted as needed, Major."

She draped her jacket carelessly over her arm and strode back to their table to get her briefcase. Today was wasted, but tomorrow would be a different story.

Because unlike her parents, she *never* relied on luck.

Chapter Seven

Rick retallied the same column of numbers for a second time. And not on purpose.

Talk about distracted.

He tossed his pencil down onto the budget spreadsheet he was supposed to be reviewing and stared out the window of the CO's office, which he was borrowing for the day. His own office right next door held a whole set of distractions of its own. He hated not being able to do his job. And no matter how hard he tried, he couldn't stop thinking about the woman who'd managed to surprise him yet again.

Surprise? She'd stunned the hell out of him.

It's amazing what you can learn when you're ten years old, sitting in the corner of a bar's poolroom, waiting for your parents' luck to run out so you can go home.

Man, he'd suspected her backbone had been earned, but not so young.

And his first, knee-jerk, gut-stupid reaction had been to rescue. To try to heal. Just as with Pete.

Rick gave a harsh laugh. Look where that had

gotten him. Right on cue, heartburn flared with a fire that would have made the spiciest food proud.

He swung the chair farther around until he faced the battalion colors displayed behind Battalion Commander Colonel Carl Bergstrom's desk. The two full-sized flags hung from staffs in brass stands, angled and crossed, the U.S. flag on the left and the Marine Corps red flag bearing his battalion's designation on the right.

Always together, as he'd thought of his future and the Marines. But to do what was right by Pete, Rick had to drastically change his plans for his future. The Marine Corps might be out, but he had his college business management degree to fall back on. His mother had been plenty eager to remind him of that when they'd met for breakfast this morning before she'd agreed to return home to San Francisco.

He swallowed down the burn and spun back toward the desk, where he straightened the papers in front of him. At least thinking about Lynn was better than thinking about his own problems.

He recalled her other revelation and the hard glint in her amber eyes when she'd explained her credo.

No ties, no limits. If I don't have any ties to anyone, I can't be limited. There will be nothing standing in my way of achieving the kind of security that doesn't go away. That can't be stripped away.

Okay, so she'd had a crappy, insecure childhood. Was security the third, "personal" goal she'd mentioned the first day? If so, how did getting him back to Dependable for the McCoys figure in with her achieving that goal? If he knew, he might be able to convince her of an alternative to messing in his life.

Assuming he could think of one.

First, he had to get her to open up to him enough that he could figure out her strategy. Then, like the survivor she was, she might be willing to form a new alliance with him rather than the McCoys.

Of course, an alliance with him would mean leaving everything well enough alone, and he wasn't sure doing so was in her nature. Why else would she continue being so persistent?

A gasp came from the doorway Rick had left open out of habit. When he'd told his men he had an open-door policy, he'd meant it. The prickling of awareness along his skin made glancing up to see who was there pointless.

"No, not you." The complaint would have been a whine from any other woman, but Southern sensuality smoothed out the edges.

Rick closed his eyes. She'd done it again. "I swear, Lynn, if you don't quit showing up when I'm thinking about you—" He almost admitted that she'd be hanging around twenty-four/seven, but she didn't need to know she was on his mind that much.

"Absolutely not," she continued as if she hadn't heard him. "You can't be here."

He opened his eyes and saw her in the doorway, shaking her head, standing there as if she'd been stopped in her tracks by the sight of him.

She'd have the same effect on any red-blooded male. Despite the distinctly pissed-off air about her—

the grip she had on her ever-present black leather briefcase would strangle just about anything, and she could bust walnuts clenching her teeth that tight—she was gorgeous.

Her longish, fitted black suit coat somehow conveyed sexuality and polished professionalism at the same time. The matching, mouth-watering, form-hugging dress beneath left miles of leg uncovered. High-heel black pumps added beckoning curves to the trip. As she shook her head, he noticed that she'd styled her hair straight and sleek, containing it with a flat silver clip of some sort at the base of her long, slender neck.

"No," she repeated.

"You said that already."

"And you're still here. Why?"

He picked up the pencil. "I'm working." At least he was supposed to be. Not obsessing on the unexpected pain in this woman's past. He shouldn't care about her pain or her past. He'd never let his interest in a woman interfere with his ability to do his job. For the simple fact that, as shallow as it sounded, his job—his career in the Marines—had always been more important to him.

Maybe she'd slipped so deep into his psyche because what was most important to him might soon be taken away.

Or maybe he'd simply never met a woman like her.

She moved farther into the office. "You're no longer the Recreational Aquatics Thermal Regulator, or whatever it was?" She almost sounded happy for him, as if she cared about what he'd been stuck with.

A rapid-fire burst of pleasure pegged him dead center. He exhaled heavily and shook his head more at himself than her. "Never was. While I'm sure it would be a lot of enlisted Marines' dream come true to see a major humiliated that way, it doesn't happen. I was being sarcastic when I told you that."

She stopped next to one of the chairs grouped around the small meeting table that, along with the brown leather couch, coffee table and a bookcase, filled the moderate-sized office. Throwing out a hip in what he was coming to know as a familiar stance, she planted a fist on the gentle swell. "You *were* being sarcastic." She shifted her weight again as if his revelation agitated her. She unfisted her hand and pointed to herself in exasperation. "And I actually felt horrible for you."

She'd felt horrible for him? He really hated how much he liked the thought of her feeling sympathetic toward him. "Yes, I was being sarcastic. Apparently, you and I have a similar coping mechanism."

"Similar *coping mechanism?*"

"We deal with stress by being smart-asses."

"Smart-alecks," she corrected, and seemed to chew on the notion for a moment. She visibly shrugged it off and asked, "Then I repeat, what are you doing in your commanding officer's office?"

"Reviewing the next fiscal-year's budget. My real temporary reassignment until my civilian problem is resolved." Which would undoubtedly lead to a permanent end to his career. The backs of his eyes burned. "And I'm working in here because Carl and I agreed it would be less awkward for the staff."

And less tempting for his unit of instructors to keep involving him in the day-to-day functioning of the Weapons Training Battalion. A couple of them had already humbled him by insisting his arrest had been a typical civi screwup and that Rick would be off the hook in no time.

If only.

Even if he and Pete continued to be the only ones who knew the truth, there was no way this could end well for him. No way at all.

The urge to howl with pain and impotency was almost too much to resist.

Lynn looked pointedly at the I-love-me wall, covered above the leather couch with plaques, certificates and photos. "Speaking of Colonel Bergstrom…"

She undoubtedly wanted to question the man about what he knew of his executive officer's behavior on and off base. Or worse yet, attempt to recruit Carl to help her get Rick to see things her way. Something Carl might be inclined to do if Rick wasn't around to convince him otherwise. He and Carl had grown close since Rick had been assigned here after recovering from his injuries, and Carl would want what was best for Rick.

So far Carl hadn't pressed him on what had happened, just offered his help any way, any how. When Rick had assured him there was nothing he needed, Carl had asked him to make sure he thought long and hard about what he was doing. If only Rick had had the chance.

Frankly, he didn't know if it would have made a difference.

Rick sat back in Carl's chair. "He's not here."

A dark eyebrow twitched. "I can see that."

"I mean he's not in the building."

She rolled her eyes. "Where is he? And don't try to tell me he shipped out, because I happen to know you guys are RBMs, which I learned means Remain-Behind-Marines."

Rick glanced at his watch. "Odds are, right now he's helping Lieutenant-Colonel Mitchell assemble one of those inflatable house things kids can jump around in for the twins' third birthday party this afternoon. Carl's famous for being handy despite his rank," Rick joked.

Carl Bergstrom was the type of Marine Rick had always intended to be, exemplifying the utmost honorability. Though Carl was in no way old enough, he was damn near a father figure to Rick.

Lynn jerked her gaze to the window, her jaw tight. One corner of her mouth tugged downward.

She was struggling for control. Until a few days ago, he wouldn't have empathized. Now he felt like a kindred spirit. To be at the mercy of others' actions wasn't easy for people like them, people used to being in control.

She brought her attention back to him. "Will he return?"

"Not today."

She glanced through the office door. The outer offices were empty, too.

Rick guessed at her train of thought. "They've all probably headed out to the birthday party already, too."

"All of them." It wasn't a question. "In the middle of a workday?"

"The twins are kind of special around here. And it was probably the only time everyone could get together."

She nodded vaguely, but he had the distinct impression she didn't really understand.

Friends get in the way.

That opinion was certainly being reinforced today. The bonds the people who worked here had formed were keeping her from getting what she wanted: the dirt on one Major Rick Branigan.

She exhaled loudly and came forward. Dropping her briefcase in one of the chairs facing the desk, she asked, "Why aren't you there?"

He'd been invited. One of the many subtle signals of support he'd received. And had to rebuke.

Because *his* friends might get in the way. They might finally press him for details of what had happened, why the police thought he had driven drunk, caused an accident, then left the scene. All things they wouldn't normally consider him capable of. Or they'd want to know what had happened to change him.

He'd told them to trust him, but he couldn't be sure how long that trust would last.

He studied Lynn and saw the hard edges she'd forged, probably out of self-preservation. He could feel the same edges forming on the already hard planes of his honorability. Another price he had to pay for making good on his debt to Pete.

"I'm not there because I'm here," he said flatly, resigned to his fate.

"Now, there's an answer."

"Yep."

Her gaze drifted to the large scheduling calendar mounted next to the window, where her attention lingered for a moment. A clock was probably ticking very loudly in her head right now. Her time was running out, thank goodness.

She contemplated the outer office again. "Lieutenant Colonel Mitchell's kids, eh?"

Rick could see her running through the ways she could get her hands on Kyle's home address. With all the people she might want to interview about Rick in one handy place, she'd hit the mother lode.

Especially if he wasn't there to interfere.

A serious tactical error on his part.

He could change his mind and go to the party so he'd be on hand in case she did decide to show up. Hell, there was no *in case*. He doubted Lynn would wait around until tomorrow to talk to the people she wanted to talk to. She'd hunt them down and corner them but good.

He might as well take her himself so he could stick close to her and keep her from probing or spurring his friends on to ask questions. Plus, he could give the twins in person the presents he'd sent along with Carl.

Rick cleared his throat to distract her from whatever plan of attack she was formulating in that beautiful head of hers. "You know, I've actually had about as much of this number crunching as I can take for now." He set aside his pencil and returned the budget spreadsheet to its file folder. "I've changed my mind. I'll go to the twins' birthday party after all."

If a look could kill, body armor wouldn't have saved him from the glare she shot his way.

He met it without blinking.

Schooling her features, she rested one hand on the back of the chair and the other on her hip. "What makes you think you'll be all that welcome? I'd think it would be a little awkward having an officer relieved of duty for a DUI hit-and-run show up at a kids' party."

"It's not a kegger, Lynn. And they're my friends." Despite what he had to ask of them, he knew in his heart that would never change. He forcibly turned his mind from all he was sacrificing.

He pushed back from the desk and stood. "And because they're my friends, they won't mind if I bring a date."

Her hand slipped off her hip. "A date?"

The choked way she repeated his offhand choice of words brought him up short. Was the thought of being something more personal to him threatening to her? Or appealing? The ego thing fired up his hormones again.

But he needed to consider his effect on her a mere advantage, nothing more. He'd ignore her effect on him—the way the moisture on her slightly parted lips made him burn to taste her, and the way the ghost of pain in her eyes tempted him to comfort her—if it killed him.

HER HEART FOOLISHLY POUNDING and her skin heating, all Lynn could do was watch the last person she'd expected—heck, the last person she'd *wanted* to encounter today—slowly come around the desk.

Her mouth went dry.

He was wearing what she assumed to be his everyday uniform—service uniform, if she remembered correctly. Khaki shirt and pants, pressed and spit-polished. Nothing special in the military world. She wouldn't be able to swing his cat around here without hitting some guy wearing the exact same thing, give or take a few medals. She knew from his file that one of the badges on his shirt was for being an expert marksman with a rifle, earned before his purple heart, which was probably stuck in a drawer. Neither was terribly unusual on this base.

But on Branigan, the uniform was somehow different.

More compelling.

Sexier.

After seeing him working out, she knew what was underneath the uniform. Acres of sculpted muscles and tanned skin, with just the right amount of dark hair on his forearms and legs to haunt her late at night.

So she shouldn't be so affected by him in uniform.

She shouldn't be a lot of things around Major Rick Branigan.

He kept coming toward her, his gaze on her mouth. Unbelievably, her lips tingled in response.

Stopping only a couple of steps away from her, he eyed her. "It's not as if I'm asking you to the senior prom, or anything."

She scoffed. This felt nothing like when she'd been asked to her senior prom. Because *nothing* was what she'd felt then. No, that wasn't entirely true. She remembered being cold and detached. The complete opposite of now. What was wrong with her?

He faltered and frowned. "Did you get to go to a prom?"

His blue eyes searched hers. He was clearly remembering what she'd revealed about her miserable childhood.

Just shoot me. Shoot me now.

Since he pretty much already knew the worst, she admitted, "Yes, I went to my senior prom. And I didn't give a rip about it because I'd been at that particular school a whopping two months and hardly knew the guy who'd asked me. But he was good for satisfying a few curiosities, so it was worth the effort." Although she'd been left feeling colder and more hollow. Another layer added to her shell.

His coal-black eyebrows dropped, but he didn't appear taken aback or appalled by her admission. "I admire your honesty."

Her heart lurched. "Wonderful."

"I have to admit that I'm curious about a few things myself." He took a step closer, bringing with him his size, his heat, the subtle spicy scent of his aftershave.

Having him near was like fighting off intoxication. Impossible.

"Welcome to the club."

That stopped him. He laughed lightly in acknowledgment that she wouldn't be any more likely to answer delving questions than he was.

He raised his devilish eyebrows at her again. "So? Do you want to come with me? I'm not sure if you'll have a chance to talk to Colonel Bergstrom, but…" He trailed off, obviously hoping she'd take the bait.

Lynn stifled another scoffing sound. She didn't believe for a second that he planned to let her talk to the colonel. He was only asking her to go with him to keep her from crashing the party on her own.

But he was not the master and commander he thought he was.

At least not when it came to her and her mission.

Trying for a look of uncertainty with a shot of insecurity, she pulled at her lip. "It's a party?" She might as well make what he'd learned about her work for her. As underhanded as her tactic might sound, manipulation was only a bad thing when it failed.

"A birthday party. For Lieutenant Colonel Kyle Mitchell's twins, Shelby and Mark."

Averting her gaze to keep from tipping her hand if he really could see through her, as he seemed able to, she fiddled with the handle of her briefcase. "And it'll just be the people you work with, right?"

"Pretty much. With their families, if they can make it."

He'd be handing to her—on a silver platter—

every person she wanted to enlist in her attempt to change his mind. Well worth the strain of his unsettling company.

Unfortunately, she feared she'd have to make that her mantra to get through the next few hours impersonally, while being Major Branigan's "date."

Chapter Eight

"Okay, scratch what I said about Carl being handy."

Lynn caught up to where Rick had stopped just around the back corner of Kyle Mitchell's modest-size, tan stucco home. Despite the swarm of people and activity in the equally modest fenced backyard, she immediately spotted what he was shaking his head at.

The inflatable house for kids to bounce around in was still far from set up, and kids of varying ages were engaged in a noisy game of chase, instead of playing in the house. The red-, blue-and-yellow house—actually more of a castle—looked like a huge balloon with a slow leak. Its netted sides drooped inward and the red turrets hung limp. Right next to the colorful castle, four men—two in uniforms exactly like Rick's and two wearing casual, short-sleeved shirts and pants—were bent over a blower of some sort that clearly wasn't doing its job of inflating the castle.

"Can't say that I see that every day," Lynn mused.

"The blow-up bounce thing or the group of highly trained Marines apparently baffled by it?"

She laughed. "Both."

He glanced down at her, his blue eyes warmed by his smile.

An answering heat spread through Lynn's chest. Something funny always happened inside her when he looked at her that way. Funny in a scary, confusing way.

He returned his attention to the castle. "Good. Then coming here with me won't have been a waste."

Abruptly, what had to have been warm pleasure chilled. Her coming here would have been a waste because he planned to keep her from talking to his commanding officer about the accident?

Not if she could help it.

One of the three women, a pretty forty-ish strawberry blonde and presumably the wife of one of the other officers, spotted them from where she stood next to a festively decorated picnic table. "Rick!"

She hurried toward them, the very image of California casual in flowy white capri pants, a coral top and matching flip-flops.

Lynn felt conspicuously overdressed, even though she'd left her jacket in her rental car. On the way over, to keep from thinking about how good Rick looked on his red-and-black, racing-type motorcycle as she followed behind him in her car, she'd decided to appear more casual, more approachable. More receptive to secrets. She hadn't considered what the dressed-down look would cost her.

As if sensing her discomfort, Rick settled his hand on the small of her back. The reassuring and decidedly possessive gesture sent an unexpected—and unwelcome—thrill through her.

He accepted the woman's hug with his free hand. She pressed a kiss to his cheek. "I'm so glad you could make it after all," she murmured before stepping back, regarding Lynn with a speculation that made Lynn more uncomfortable.

Rick answered, "I decided some things shouldn't be missed."

Lynn pressed her lips together. *Especially things he needed to control,* she thought sourly.

He chose that moment to turn to her and she had to quickly school her features.

"Sue, this is a friend of mine—Lynn Hayes."

Thrown off by his calling her his friend, Lynn offered her hand. At least he hadn't called her his date. She ignored the faint prick of disappointment. She must be losing it.

"Lynn, meet Sue Mitchell, the mother of the Miraculous Twins, as they're known around here."

Lynn looked from one to the other. "Miraculous?" Sounded a little ominous.

Sue smiled broadly as she shook Lynn's hand. "We were at a base function when I went into premature labor with them. And even though I had tried for so long to get pregnant, they were in a big fat hurry to be born." She waved a hand at the men fiddling with the blower fan and the women either arranging food on the picnic table or riding herd on the

kids. "Pretty much everyone here is acquainted a little more intimately with me than I'd prefer."

Sue laughed and patted Rick's chest. "But fortunately, this big guy is so hot-blooded. He kept Shelby,
who was the tiniest, warm by tucking her right inside
his dress-uniform shirt, against his skin, until they
could get her into an incubator. She was all...well,
icky. Not every fella would be willing to do something like that."

Rick's gaze landed on Lynn's only briefly before
skipping away. He had to be aware what was running
through her mind. A guy who'd think to hold a newborn baby like that would be very unlikely to walk
away from an injured person, even if he'd been the
one to cause the injury.

She didn't buy his guilt for a second.

Sue took ahold of his arm and tugged him forward. "Come on, join the party. Shelby will be so
pleased to see you." To Lynn, she said, "Ever since
she first heard the story of her birth, Shelby has considered Rick hers."

His hand still on her back, urging her along with
them so she had to pick her way through the grass in
her black pumps, Rick dipped his head close to
Lynn's. "More like a pet than anything else."

Sue overheard him and laughed again. "True. Or
her own personal jungle gym. But that's as much
your fault as it is hers."

"Hey, I can't help it if her father treats her like a
porcelain doll and doesn't let her roughhouse the
way he does her brother. The girl needs to get it out

of her system now and again." This time Rick whispered to Lynn, "I bought her a baseball mitt and squishy ball. Her brother got the plastic bat." He winked to confirm this unexpected mischievous streak in him that upped his attractiveness tenfold.

Just what Lynn needed.

The girl who she assumed to be the one in question—a miniature version of Sue, only with more delicate features and tight strawberry-blond curls—let out a high-pitched squeal of delight at the sight of Rick. No wonder her father treated her so differently from her brother; she resembled a fragile doll, complete with a frilly white party dress.

Right until she ran up and launched herself at him.

He stepped forward and deftly caught her, then promptly spun her upside down and back around so fast that her dress didn't have a chance to flip up.

The scene was straight out of a Kodak-film commercial. Incredibly handsome man with a beautiful, precious little girl he obviously adored at a picture-perfect party—the droopy castle added charm—on a picture-perfect early-summer day.

All of it far from Lynn's realm of experience.

All of it something she'd at one point or another in her life dreamed of. Maybe even wished for.

All so counter to what her brain told her she really needed.

"Rick—" Shelby was giggling so hard she could barely say his name as he set her bare feet back on the ground. The fact that she had dirty feet and similar smudges on her lace-trimmed dress helped make her seem more normal kid than doll.

Rick tweaked her nose. "Happy b-day, Shel."

A little boy in long khaki shorts and a Spider Man T-shirt ran up to Rick. He bore enough of a resemblance to Shelby to have to be Mark, the twin brother, despite being quite a bit bigger. "Presents! Have to have presents!"

"Mark!" his mother admonished.

Moving so quickly he surprised them all, Rick snatched Mark up and turned him upside down, too; only, he held the little boy that way against his broad chest, making Mark belly-laugh and his face turn red.

"Your presents from me are already here, squirt. The colonel brought them with him."

"'Kay! 'Kay!" Mark gasped between laughs. "You can come to the party."

"Good, because I'm already here." Rick flipped him right-side up and dumped him on his feet.

Lynn stared, her heart in her throat. She never, ever would have guessed that a quintessential leatherneck like Rick, so stiff in his honor and duty, could be so at ease, so *wonderful* with children. The man was born to be a father.

Something that would prove difficult to impossible from behind bars. Based on her experience, the world was in short supply of decent fathers capable of these kinds of moments as it was.

Good Lord, she *had* to do something about the charges against him.

Mark straightened his shirt with amazing dignity

for a three-year-old. But then, he was the son of a Marine. "Can you help Dad get the house up?" he asked, with equally amazing clarity, and pointed at the castle. "We can't jump unless it's all the way up."

"I'll give it a try. If I can't, I'm sure my friend Lynn here—" he canted a thumb toward her "—can blow it up the old-fashioned way."

"Yay!" the twins said in unison before racing off toward the kids hovering near the bowls of chips and other snacks.

A hint of the warm pleasure returned and crept beneath her skin at being included in his teasing. "Are you implying I'm full of hot air, Major?"

"Ooh." Sue laughed. "I hope you two are *good* friends, or you're going to find yourself with nothing but the Corps for a date again, Rick." She moved over to nudge Lynn with her elbow. "A crying shame, if I may say so."

Rick grumbled, "No, you may not."

Sue blew him a kiss and turned back to Lynn. "Why don't you come with me and I'll get you something to drink while you tell me how you came to know our Rick."

Strong fingers closed gently but firmly around Lynn's elbow as Rick stepped into her space. "Sorry, but she's coming with me. I'm not joking when I say she's smarter than all your bouncy-house repair crew combined. She'll help me earn points with the boss men."

Her earlier hint of warmth erupted into a full-out flush at his possessiveness. Her brain shouted that he was simply keeping her from having a chance to talk to anyone without him near.

Her body didn't care.

Sue's eyebrows inched upward with speculation. And blatant delight. "Okay." To Rick she said, "I know you'll want a beer." To Lynn, she added, "Can I get you one, too? Or a soda or lemonade?"

"Lemonade would be great, thank you."

Sue nodded. "I'll bring them over to you." She headed for the picnic table. The other women had paused in their bustling around the food-laden spread and were looking their way, making comments.

Lynn was *so* out of her element. Self-consciousness doused everything else and helped her refocus on her purpose.

In a low voice she said to Rick, "She's certain you'll want a beer because you drink a lot of it?" Even as she said it, she knew in her gut the supposition couldn't be true. But maybe if she kept at him, he'd slip up eventually and say something she could use to figure out the truth.

He gestured to the other men, who were also now mostly watching her and Rick. "She's certain I'll want a beer because it's a required tool around here when there's 'some assembly required.'"

Lynn allowed him to start leading her toward the half-inflated inflatable house. She appreciated the fact that he didn't rush her across the grass in her high heels. She must look ridiculous. But she had to do what she had to do.

One of the men in casual clothes—a subtle Hawaiian-print coral shirt and tan shorts—raised his beer bottle at their approach. "Glad you could find your way here after all, Branigan."

Rick pointed at the older man's shirt. "Sue dressing you again, Kyle?"

"That's an affirmative." He smiled at Lynn and stepped forward, his free hand outstretched. "Lieutenant Colonel Kyle Mitchell, unfortunate new owner of one defective Castle Bounce."

Lynn shook his hand, his grip sure and friendly. "Lynn Hayes, couns—"

"You bought the thing? Whatever happened to renting?" Rick cut her off before she could add her title at McCoy Enterprises.

Kyle released Lynn's hand and spread his arms in an expansive shrug. "I get in those warehouse stores and lose my objective."

The other casually dressed man, in a blue shirt and khaki pants, said, "You mean you lose your common sense."

He was the shortest and probably the oldest, at least in his late forties or early fifties, but it was hard to tell because of the men's closely cropped hair, dark tans and muscular, fit bodies.

Tipping his beer bottle toward Rick, he said, "My XO—or executive officer—needs to work on his manners," and reached a hand out to Lynn, too. "Colonel Carl Bergstrom, ma'am. It's a pleasure to meet you."

"Pleasure meeting you, too." As she shook his strong, square hand, she dared to add, "I'm sorry I missed you earlier."

Graying sandy brows went up.

Rick said, "Sorry."

Presumably apologizing for his failure to introduce Lynn to the rest of the men, but also neatly keeping the colonel from commenting on what she'd said.

Rick gestured toward the other two uniformed officers. "Lynn, Major Bill Stuttelford and Lieutenant Jay Crane."

She shook each man's hand and acknowledged them, finally feeling more in her element. While she did enjoy working with several women—Sara Barnes, VP of Operations in particular—she realized she was most comfortable dealing with the men.

Most likely because they were her competition. She thrived on competition. And generally she could anticipate how men would react to any given situation.

Rick was the notable exception. He'd confounded her from the start. She was far from comfortable around him, for more reasons than she cared to consider.

Considering them gave them weight.

Not willing to lose their attention, she asked, "You all work together?"

The lieutenant—young, attractive, no wedding ring, thankfully, because he was giving her legs the once-over—jumped to answer. "Yes, ma'am."

Rick warned, "The 'ma'ams' will get you nowhere fast, Jay."

Kyle toed the blue metal box containing the blower fan. "Just like where we're getting with this thing. Why don't you take a look at it, Rick."

Rick cast a glance at her that only she'd note as

assessing. She smiled sweetly at him, and his expression darkened. Having little choice, he squatted next to the silent blower anyway and started poking and prodding.

Jay took Rick's place next to her. "So how long have you known Rick?"

Rick straightened and asked Jay, "Is it still plugged in?"

The other men exchanged blank looks, then laughed.

Jay grinned and wagged a finger at Rick. "Now see, that's why you made major so soon."

Something he probably wouldn't be for long.

The joviality leaked from the group the same way the air had leaked from the inflatable house. It was a real indication of how these people felt about Rick. She dearly hoped he realized how fortunate he was.

Rick's expression shifted only slightly, and if she hadn't known what to watch for—the pain and frustration he'd shown her the first day they met—she would have missed the shadow in his eyes.

The awkward silence lasted only seconds before Kyle called, "Sue?"

"Yeah, hon?" his wife answered, coming toward them carrying a glass of lemonade in one hand and a beer in the other.

"Will you check to see if that extension cord has been accidentally pulled out of the socket?"

She stopped and turned back toward the house. "Mark, honey? Can you check to see if the castle is plugged in, please?" she called, relaying the request to her son despite his young age. The trickle-down theory in action.

The little boy ran over to the exterior outlet next to the sliding-glass door into the house. "Still plugged in!" he hollered back.

Rick asked, "What about the breaker?"

Kyle nodded. "You're right. The blower could have tripped the breaker, especially if someone had turned on something in the house on the same circuit." He sighed and trudged toward the house, earning a kiss on the cheek from his wife as he passed her.

When Sue reached Lynn and Rick, she handed them their drinks. "And here I'd thought we bought that silly thing for the kids to play with."

Colonel Bergstrom chuckled as he moved to stand between Lynn and Rick. "Sue, can I trouble you for another one of those beers?"

"Sure, Carl." Sue turned and retraced her steps.

Lynn noticed the colonel still had a good half of his beer left in the dark amber bottle in his hand. She raised a brow.

To the other two officers, he said, "Jay, Bill, why don't you guys get the barbecue fired up and the hot dogs going. Those kids are only going to wait to eat for so long. And if Kyle doesn't come out soon, go make sure he hasn't shut off the power to the refrigerator, or something similarly important."

"Can do, sir," Jay said, and the two men headed for the part of the patio where the gas grill sat against the back of the house.

As soon as they were out of earshot, which didn't

have to be far, considering the noise the playing kids were making, the colonel trained his steel-gray eyes on her and said, "So, you're the lawyer who has been wanting to talk to me about my man here?"

"Yes. That would be me." She resisted the urge to check Rick's reaction to the news that she'd tried to get ahold of his commanding officer prior to showing up at his office. His failure to take or return her calls was what had prompted her visit in the first place.

Gripping her iced lemonade in hands sweating more than the glass in the warm sun, Lynn again wished she hadn't left her suit coat in the rental car. She'd feel more like herself. More in control. More protected.

The colonel studied Rick. "Any changes I should be aware of?"

"No, sir. None whatsoever."

"Good enough."

Rick had outmaneuvered her. Lynn gaped at the two men. They were shutting her out completely, as slick as that.

"Colonel Bergstrom." She looked the older man straight in the eye. "I've been sent by the major's family to help him. And I'm not being egotistical in saying I am qualified for the job. Just because he is being bullheaded about this doesn't mean you shouldn't help me help him."

He frowned and turned to Rick. "Your mother hired her?"

"She works for my father's family. Who just happen to be the people who own the McCoy stores."

This time Lynn nearly gasped, and pursed her lips to keep from making a sound. She hadn't expected him to tell anyone about the McCoys, even though his connection to them was bound to make the news at some point.

Another ticking bomb set to go off if she didn't get him free and clear of his legal troubles. She needed to unearth the truth and exonerate him quickly. Or, if Rick did turn out to be guilty, she needed to get the DA to accept a guilty or *nolo contendere*—no contest—plea to a lesser charge before Rick had any notoriety attached to him.

Overall, the colonel appeared only mildly interested, but his eyes were sharp on Rick. "Your father? Hmm. So something *has* changed."

Lynn glanced at Rick. He wasn't all secrets with everyone, it seemed. Something twisted painfully inside her. She'd never had anyone to share deeply personal things with. Ever. She felt even more the emotional vagrant.

On the upside, she wouldn't have to tiptoe around the whole truth now when talking to the colonel about Rick. Maybe being aware of what Rick had waiting for him in Dependable would sway the colonel toward helping her. The prospect made her heart pound against her ribs. She might have this in the bag yet.

Rick shrugged as if his paternity wasn't any big deal, but his jaw tensed. "The guy died and, for whatever reason, acknowledged me in his will. Miss Hayes—" his blue eyes lit on her for the barest of moments, but long enough to reveal the shadows there despite his casual tone "—who is one of the McCoy-family lawyers—"

She interjected, "Actually, I work for the McCoys' corporation, McCoy Enterprises." Working solely for the family was her ultimate goal, as a partner in the elite Weidman, Biddermier, Stark law firm. The reminder brought the steel back to her spine. "At the moment."

Rick regarded her more fully, one of his eyebrows ticking upward, before meeting the colonel's steady gaze again. "Anyway, she was sent to deliver the news."

Surprise flickered across the colonel's face, but before he could comment, Lynn added, "And to get him out of his legal mess as quickly and quietly as possible so he can come to Dependable, Missouri, in time for his grandfather's seventy-fifth birthday party, then execute the terms of his father's—Marcus McCoy's—will."

The colonel asked, "Which is?"

Lynn rushed to answer. "To take his rightful place in the family and family business."

Colonel Bergstrom pulled his chin in. "Really?" he mused more than asked. "Interesting." He looked at Rick. "And something more likely to happen now."

Meaning now that Rick was about to be out of a career, he'd be free to go to Dependable.

Unless he ended up in jail.

Lynn's heart pounded harder. If anyone could sway Rick, the man he clearly respected could. "But only if he lets me help him, which he won't."

Rick's gaze slid back to her. "Lynn," he warned.

Colonel Bergstrom crossed his arms over his chest and scrutinized Rick's face.

Rick stood there the way he had the first day she'd met him. Stubborn. Taciturn. And utterly unimpressed by the McCoys' billions.

The colonel inhaled and exhaled, deep and slow, his chest expanding and contracting beneath his arms. He gave a short nod. Decision made. "Well, I've only known this Marine to make one mistake." He focused on Lynn. "If he's doing what he thinks is best at the moment, I'll support him until he tells me to do otherwise."

Lynn did gasp this time. Why would the colonel allow Rick to screw up so bad? Bergstrom was making the DUI hit-and-run sound like some sort of brain burp, the same as shaking the salad dressing bottle without the lid on tight. But this was one colossal mess that Rick shouldn't be allowed to try to clean up on his own.

Especially when he was most likely innocent.

Chapter Nine

Rick watched Lynn try to process Carl's loyalty, and sympathy stirred in his chest. If she thought friends only got in the way, then she'd have a hard time understanding how his friends—Carl being one of his closest—could so loyally help him achieve what he wanted. Without questioning or second-guessing.

Rick knew they were very worried about him, especially since a civil conviction of any kind—if it didn't get him discharged or demoted—would nevertheless keep him from moving up in rank. He'd have to leave the Corps after twenty years of service, regardless. But his friends would trust that he was doing what he was doing for a damn good reason, and leave it at that.

If they found out he was sacrificing his career for a debt owed to Pete Wright, however, Rick might have a fight on his hands. It was a given that Marines save each other's lives. No payback expected. But no one else knew about the demons from Pete's past that still nipped at his heels. No one else would understand.

Certainly not Lynn Hayes.

He noticed she gripped her glass of lemonade so tightly the condensation moisture was beading on her fingers. She might not understand, but she wouldn't let it go. The ache of sympathy turned to the warmth of an ever-growing admiration for her. She was a fighter, this one.

Before she could pick a fight with Carl, Rick claimed her elbow again, very aware of how easy it had become for him to touch her. The usual barriers he put up to keep from forming additional attachments he didn't have the time to properly maintain didn't exist with her. Probably because of what they understood about each other, the glimpses they had of what drove each other, thanks to the emotional volatility of the situation they'd been thrust into together.

Although he still couldn't fathom why the truth was so important to her. Distracting her with a little physical encroachment had worked before. Maybe he should find the opportunity to try it again.

He said, "As interesting as my problems may be, how about we go check out the food?"

Her eyes glowed virtually gold with resolve. "I didn't come here to eat, Rick."

"No big surprise there. But this isn't the time."

The fan on the multicolored castle's inflator kicked on as if to add an exclamation point to what he'd said. The noise startled Lynn—he still had ahold of her elbow and felt her jump. The fan also would have drowned out anything she might have said in return, so she didn't try.

Kyle emerged from the house and raised his hands

in triumph. The contraption must have tripped the electrical breaker.

The kids squealed in delight and ran to the entrance of the bouncing house, lining up for their turns. They took up a chant of encouragement as the castle turrets slowly straightened and the jumping platform puffed up with air.

Carl gestured that he intended to move as far away from the noise as possible. Rick waved at him to go ahead.

A corner of Lynn's mouth pulled downward as she watched Carl walk away, but an ironic smirk quickly replaced her frustration "tell."

She shouted, "Saved by the blower?"

Rick leaned close so she'd be sure to hear him. "Occasionally, I do get lucky." He caught a whiff of her perfume and the urge to bury his nose in her midnight-dark hair overwhelmed him.

He *needed* some luck when it came to her. Especially if he intended to establish the barriers between them that definitely needed establishing should he survive getting close to her again. Because even if he hadn't decided to spend this time in his life focused on his career, his current situation—and her part in it—made anything that might develop between them impossible.

The knowledge rested heavily on his chest and shoulders, as if a part of him wished otherwise. More than just the part that the sight, smell and feel of her made randy. But he could handle it. In this, at least, he was in control.

He gently urged her away from the blower and ever-fattening castle, soon to be filled with bouncing kids. "Let's see if the hot dogs are going yet."

She came along for a few paces until they were far enough from the noise that they could hear themselves think, then halted. For a moment she watched the cluster of smiling, laughing adults who occasionally threw curious glances their way.

She pried one hand off her lemonade glass and wiped it on her hip several times. "I'm not really in a hot-dog mood."

A full-scale retreat? So soon? Disappointment ran him over like a tank.

She slipped out of his grasp. "Go do the man-and-fire thing with the other guys. I'll just talk with the ladies."

Stupidly relieved she wasn't giving up so easily, he smiled at her. "And do some grilling of your own, right?"

Her quirked brow and mouth said, *Yeah, so?*

He reached for her free hand and tucked it in the crook of his arm, starting them moving forward again. "Actually, I've always preferred the company of women."

"Then why don't you have one of your own by now?" The question had a sharp edge to it.

Jealousy? His pulse surged at the prospect. So much for control. Her fingers moved with an uneasy grip on his arm, igniting a prickling awareness throughout his whole body.

Or was she questioning the attraction so obviously stirring between them?

This was one question she deserved to have answered honestly, not only out of respect and admiration but to help get those barriers up. "This sounds cliché, but I don't have a woman of my own because I haven't found the right one yet. One willing to support my commitment to the Corps."

In that disconcerting way she had, she looked right into him. "You mean you haven't found a woman willing to be second best with you."

He opened his mouth to automatically deny the accusation, but snapped it shut. His psyche was taking enough of a beating lately without questioning the sort of man he'd become. "If that was the case, it's a moot point now."

"I suppose so. It wouldn't exactly be the honorable thing to get involved with a woman while you're well on your way to being sent up the river, so to speak. Not to say there aren't women who go for the whole 'jailbird sweethearts' thing."

He snorted a laugh as they reached the three other women, swarming as women do when there is food to be served and there are children to manage. Unfortunately, the idea of becoming involved with a woman led him to thinking about being involved with the woman on his arm.

All that silky dark hair, those legs...not to mention everything in between. Heat exploded low in his gut.

A dumb idea if he'd ever had one, and the very antithesis of establishing walls between them.

Sue, who'd already waited on Carl, and the two other wives left what they were doing to greet them.

Lynn slipped her hand from his arm and stepped sideways away from him.

Diana said, "Hey, Rick!" She gripped his forearm and gave him a quick kiss on the cheek, easily done because of her height.

He murmured, "What, no marathon to run today?"

"That will be tomorrow after I pig out on birthday cake."

Angela tucked her chin-length, light brown hair behind her ears and stepped over to hug him, squeezing tight. "It's so good to see you, hon."

They were worried about him. He could see it in their eyes, feel it in their touch.

He gave them both a *trust me* look. "Ladies." He gestured to Lynn. "I'd like you to meet a new friend of mine, Lynn Hayes. Came all the way from Dependable, Missouri, for a quick visit."

Well-traveled Corps wives all, they all murmured "oh" and nodded.

"Lynn, this is Angela Bergstrom, Carl's commanding officer," he said.

Angela swatted him. "I wish. It's a true pleasure to meet you, Lynn, and welcome to California."

Lynn nodded to her. "Thank you. I'm really enjoying the cool breeze off the ocean. Something we definitely don't have in Dependable."

Angela cocked her head. "Say, isn't that where the family who owns that big retail chain, McCoys, is located? I heard something about them on an entertainment show last night."

Rick inwardly groaned. The last thing he needed was to go there with them. Carl knowing was one thing—

Lynn nodded again. "Yes, it is. And I work for them."

Before they headed any further down that mine-strewn road, Rick extended a hand toward the woman he'd yet to introduce. "And that's Diane Stuttelford, Bill's wife and the brave woman willing to claim four of the jumping beans over there as her own." He jerked a thumb at the castle.

Diane laughed. "Some days, and only because they're all carbon copies of their father. It's a pleasure to meet you, Lynn." She came forward and offered Lynn her hand.

Lynn smiled graciously and shook it. "The resemblance has to be an amazing coincidence, because with your figure, you must have adopted."

Diane said, "Pee-shaw" and waved off the compliment, yet beamed.

Rick doubted Lynn had heard his marathon comment to Diane, but if she had, he was impressed by how she'd managed to acknowledge all the time and effort Diane put into remaining fit.

Diane inspected Lynn's perfect figure, accented by the tailored fit of the sleeveless dress that had made his jaw drop after she shed her suit coat. "You sure don't look like you've had any kids."

Lynn shook her head. "No, I haven't."

Sue caught the thread of the conversation and butted in. "Husband?"

"No, no husband. I'm pretty much married to my work."

There she went, trying to redirect the conversation to her job. The reason for her being here. The reason, he suspected, behind everything she did.

"Really?" Sue didn't take her eyes off Lynn, but Rick could hear in her tone the matchmaking machinery gearing up.

In his head he ran through about five of his best swear words.

Angela grinned. "We happen to be acquainted with someone just like that."

Four pairs of eyes turned his way, three sly and speculative, one guarded.

He waved an imaginary white flag. "Okay, enough of that. Do you have any burgers or salmon to go on the barbecue? Or did Shelby and Mark insist on coming up with the menu?"

Sue rolled her eyes. "What do *you* think?"

Rick shrugged at Lynn. "Sorry, we're stuck with hot dogs."

Her gaze darted to Sue, then the ground. "That's okay. No problem." Her cheeks flushed red.

Turbo hostess replaced matchmaker in a flash. Sue raised a staying hand to Lynn. "Oh, you don't have to eat hot dogs! I can get you something else, no problem."

Lynn's laugh was self-conscious. "It's fine, I promise."

But Sue wouldn't be put off, never able, he'd learned, to bear the thought of someone at her house going hungry. She started rattling off the contents of her refrigerator.

While Sue occupied Lynn, Diane stepped close to him, an ominous expression on her face. "Bill and I bumped into Pete the other day."

Rick's throat seized. Diane knew they'd served together and been friends—all of them at the party knew—but he prayed she wasn't aware of how much history he and Pete had together. She shouldn't, because he'd never talked to Bill about it, so he couldn't have passed the information on to his wife.

But Pete might have. Damn.

She met his gaze, her green eyes troubled. "He was his usual joking self, but he didn't look so good, Rick. Has he been—?"

Rick held up a hand to stop her from saying fighting, or drinking or both. "I know."

He glanced at Lynn and found her watching him as she answered Sue, saying she would be more than happy to eat hot dogs and potato salad. He wasn't sure if she could hear Diane, let alone follow two conversations at once, but he wasn't going to risk that she could.

Besides, he didn't want Diane or Bill to think enough about Pete's current state to mention something to Carl, who'd definitely start speculating about the timing of Pete's injuries and Rick's arrest.

Hoping to reassure Diane enough to put Pete out of her mind, he said, "I've talked to him, and everything is okay."

"Really? Oh, good. Because with a baby on the way and everything…"

Rick nodded and, thank God, noticed Diane and Bill's second youngest child sneaking a T-shirt full of barbecue Doritos back toward the bounce castle.

Rick pointed at the boy. "I think Charlie's found a way to pack his own field rations."

Diane's eyes went wide. "Oh, my goodness. Charlie! Not in your white shirt! It'll be orange now. And certainly not that many before you have a hot dog." She grabbed a paper plate off the table.

Charlie giggled and took off running.

Diane started after the wily six-year-old, and turned her ankle in her wedged sandals. "Bill—" She started to pass the buck, but her husband had his hands full of paper plates loaded with the first hot dogs and buns to come off the grill. She growled and squatted to remove her sandals.

Rick checked on Lynn. She was shifting her attention from him to Sue to Angela, who'd joined in the challenge of finding something for Lynn to eat.

He made a grumbling noise of his own. "Don't take off your shoes, Diane. I'll get him, Doritos and all."

Diane heaved a sigh. "Thanks, Rick. You're the best."

With one last glance at Lynn—her return stare appeared agonized—he began stalking a mischievous and thoroughly delighted little boy, intending to get back within earshot of Lynn as quickly as possible.

Lynn was upset, either because she wasn't discovering anything useful to her cause or because she sadly didn't possess the skills to handle hanging out with the people he'd been blessed to have in his life for the past three years.

People he'd soon have to live without.

Eventually, he'd have to cut himself off from them to protect them from the stain of association. Pain of his own stabbed his chest. The costs of what he was doing for Pete kept piling up.

Maybe both he and Lynn needed to give themselves a break and get out of here. He could then make a concerted effort to find out what was up with her, and hopefully figure out a way to counter it.

He put an end to the chase game, snagged Charlie around the waist below his chip stash and hoisted him up. Normally, the tangy barbecue smell of the chips would have sent him straight for the bowl to get a shirtful of his own, but he wasn't in the mood.

It was the first time a woman had managed to make him lose his appetite.

And a reason to erect some fortifications between them if there ever was one.

HER WHOLE BODY ACHING in a way she'd never experienced before, Lynn watched Rick carry Diane's stout, squirming little boy back to her as if he weighed no more than a wiggly kitten.

The steel-spined Marine was simply amazing with children.

And with his friends, she thought as he distracted the boy by pointing up at the fluffy white contrail of a long-gone jet so Diane could dump the chips out of his shirt onto a paper plate. Sue excused herself and rushed to help.

Children and friends. Two things she'd never given much thought to before, because they didn't pertain to her plan for her life. Noticing them now, through Rick, seemed especially bittersweet.

"Isn't he the best?"

Angela's sighed praise reminded Lynn with a jolt that she wasn't alone.

"Uh, yeah." Lynn straightened and got back to business. "Except when it comes to seeing to his own interests."

"That's the truth. The man would do anything for his friends. Above and beyond the usual Corps loyalty. Which is saying something, because the man is as gungy as they get."

Lynn turned to give the older woman her full attention. "Gungy?"

"Oh, sorry. *Gungy* is short for *gung-ho,* which is Chinese for 'working together.' You know, like *esprit de corps. Gung-ho* has been a rallying cry for Marines since World War II, along with *Semper Fi.*

"Anyway—" Angela waved away her slip into tour-guide mode. "They use *gungy* to describe a squared-away, hard-charging Marine who lives and breathes the Corps. And not in a nice way occasionally, if it's become an obsession. Rick wasn't quite there. Yet."

"And he never will be, sitting in jail." What will he do without the driving force in his life? What would she do without her job? The thought almost made her shudder.

The colonel's wife shifted and seemed to consider Lynn in a new light, much the way her husband had. "So you know about what's going on with him?"

"I'm trying to. I'm a lawyer and I want to help him." *Need to help him,* she mentally corrected herself. For his sake as well as hers.

"I figured you were some sort of professional…because of your outfit."

Lynn self-consciously smoothed a hand down the front of her fitted suit dress. "I was planning to interview Colonel Bergstrom—your husband—today, not attend a party. It was wonderful of Sue and you all to welcome me, by the way."

Angela surprised Lynn by reaching for her hand and giving it a squeeze. "Of course we would. Rick has always been such a good judge of people." Lines formed at the corners of her mouth and her gaze drifted to Rick, still holding on to Charlie while Diane and Sue tried to wipe off his shirt. "Most of the time."

Lynn's instincts flared again.

Before she could figure out what question to ask, Angela sighed, and it sounded as if it'd come from the very pit of her soul. "I've been praying nonstop that everything works out for him."

"I could help make that happen, but he won't let me."

Angela's impeccably shaped, light brown brows slammed together, and then her expression softened. She shook her head sadly. "If that's what he wants, we have to respect his decision."

Lynn clenched her teeth. Another dead end.

Angela exhaled heavily again. "He must have a very, very good reason for doing what he's doing."

Lynn's gaze was pulled back to the man. "Or so he thinks."

Also watching Rick as he set Charlie free and started toward them with Sue, Angela said softly, "More than anyone else I know, Rick deserves to be happy. He deserves to have the career he loves and a wife and kids of his own to share his life with." Her attention shifted to her husband. "Oh, no. Now Carl is in the chips. Definitely not low-carb. If you'll excuse me…" Her voice trailed off as she went to shoo the colonel away from the snacks, establishing the hierarchy.

Lynn swallowed hard. Realization hit her as to why the thought of Rick with a family of his own affected her so.

Good Lord.

The ache throbbing through her was yearning.

Chapter Ten

Struggling to regain her equilibrium, Lynn pasted on what she hoped was her usual boardroom smile—noncommittal, emotionally ambiguous, but most important, self-assured.

After Rick had searched her face for only a moment his sensual mouth and vivid blue eyes softened.

Rats. She hadn't pulled it off. Or worse yet, he could see through her.

No.

The shell that had developed over so many years was thicker than that. She'd been considered nothing more than an irritant by her parents, and layer after layer had formed over her, the same way a pearl forms.

But there was nothing lustrous or coveted about her, and she'd been spat out like so much grit.

"How about we head out?" Rick suggested, absently tucking behind her ear a strand of hair that had slipped from its clip.

Her skin tingled, sharp and hot. That, coupled with the heavy weight of Sue's interest, created an irrational need to stick around long enough to prove there was nothing romantic between her and Rick.

She brought her chin up a notch. "Don't you want to stay to see Shelby and Mark open your presents to them?"

He shook his head. "Kyle will be looking for some payback for contributing to Shelby's tomboy tendencies by giving her sports equipment."

Sue chuckled and nodded. "You're probably right about that."

Lynn objected, "There's nothing 'tomboy' about a baseball and mitt! Though a softball might have been a better choice—to get her used to catching and throwing a larger ball. Not to say she can't play baseball with the boys if she wants to."

He smiled crookedly and took a sizable chunk out of her shell. "A ball player, eh? You probably opted to give the boys a run for their money, didn't you."

The pain living in her heart slipped out and repaired the chink. "No, I didn't."

The only sport she'd played as a child was "run away," emotionally and, occasionally, physically. Not until her early teens had she decided it was time to stand and fight or risk getting sucked into the same spiral of failure and destruction as her parents. It had nearly cost her everything.

Sue touched Lynn's arm. "You two don't have to stay. Rick's golden with Shelby for just showing up." She looked to Rick, her face beaming with encouragement. "Why don't you go grab a bite down at Dock's. Watch the sunset."

Lynn blanched. Did her yearning for Rick show?

He rolled his eyes. "Please don't start with me now, Sue," he said, sounding put-upon.

Sue raised her hands and stepped back. "It's just a suggestion. But go ahead and take off. I wasn't expecting you, so I bought turkey dogs."

Rick groaned and tilted his head back. "Not turkey dogs. Hot dogs should be made out of unidentifiable *beef* parts, not turkey parts."

"Yes, I know how you feel about turkey dogs. Even though parts are parts." She moved behind him so she could give him a gentle shove toward the side yard they'd come through when they arrived. "So go. It's okay. I'll tell everyone bye for you."

To Lynn she said, "It was wonderful meeting you, and I hope we get to see you again. You two are just gorgeous together."

Lynn didn't know quite what to say to that, so she smiled and waved as she started toward the side yard. Whether Rick was coming or not, she wanted to leave. His seemingly endless string of devoted friends was a stark and surprisingly painful contrast to her own emotional isolation.

An isolation she knew to be her best defense against being hurt again. She couldn't forget that.

"Sorry about Sue."

Startled that Rick was so close behind her, Lynn snagged her heel in the lawn. She would have twisted her ankle, but he caught her around the waist with both hands and easily kept her from tumbling sideways.

"Careful there," he murmured.

"Uh, thanks." She expected him to release her, but he left one hand firmly on her waist. How could his touch be so strong yet so gentle at the same time? How could she feel the heat of his hand through the lined material of her suit dress? How could he make her feel so cared for so easily?

It's all in your head, you nitwit.

This friends-and-family stuff was getting to her. First Joseph McCoy's grief from the loss of his son, then his subsequent joy over discovering he had three more grown grandsons he was determined to have near. Now Rick and his parade of blindly faithful friends. It was almost enough to make a girl want to belong somewhere.

Almost.

Clamping the lid down on all the mushy sentiment, she stepped firmly away from Rick's hand. "Why do you feel you have to apologize for Sue?"

"For her running us off to go watch the sunset together."

Lynn stepped gratefully onto the sidewalk in front of the Mitchells' house and shrugged. "It's not uncommon for married women to indulge in a little matchmaking. Helps minimize the temptations on all sides."

Though from what Lynn could tell, Sue—the other ladies, too—appeared to genuinely care about Rick's happiness, and to be worried about his dedication to the Corps. At least the latter would be alleviated sooner rather than later. They should be pushing him toward Lynn because she was a lawyer, not because "they looked gorgeous together."

Rick scoffed. "Sue's not minimizing temptation. She's rising to a challenge. Has been since I was first assigned to the same unit as Kyle."

And probably instantly became friends with the family... There were people Lynn had worked with at McCoy Enterprises for years and she still didn't know if they were married, let alone know their spouses' names.

What did that say about her?

It said she took care of herself; that was what. Something Rick needed a crash course in.

Rick reached her rental car first and opened the door for her, correctly guessing she hadn't locked it. If stuff wasn't safe surrounded by Marine officers, it wasn't safe anywhere.

He settled his forearms on the top of the door and leaned his weight on them. "She flat-out told me once that she considers me the Mount Everest of matchmaking challenges and has been on the look-out for my—" he made quotation marks in the air with his fingers "—'soulmate.'"

Unaccountably, Lynn's heart started to pound. She blamed it on the fact that he appeared so at ease, so much more open to her than he'd ever been, walking close to him to get into the car struck her as dangerous.

And tempting.

Before she could make the move to climb in, he continued, speaking softly. "Since I did, at some point, want to take that next step in life and have a family—" he made a vague gesture toward the tidy two-story houses lining the street on both sides, echoing with the squeals of happy children "—I've gone along with her efforts, for the most part."

This time without derision, she said, "To find the woman who'd support your commitment to the Marines."

His attention on his Lieutenant Colonel's house, he nodded.

She rested the heel of her hand on the roof and struggled for objectivity. Maybe she'd been going about this all wrong. Maybe he'd been at Rancho Margarita with a woman. "A female Marine would be the logical choice."

He shook his head. "Gets tough coordinating assignments. And if the relationship doesn't work out, it's tougher to have to work together afterward."

"Voice of experience?"

"Not personally. But I've seen it often enough."

His gaze searched hers, pulling her in, making her forget everything but how beautifully blue his eyes were.

"What about you? What are you looking for, Lynn?"

The next promotion.

And the next and the next until she finally felt secure.

She inhaled deeply and slapped on an admittedly weak smile. "My next meal, actually. How far away is this 'Doctor's' Sue mentioned?"

He straightened away from the car door. "Not Doc's. The kind with boats."

"Ah. A *k*. Right. Is it far? I just realized I'm starved."

He nodded at the Mitchells'. "We could go back around and have hot dogs."

She smiled when he all but shuddered. "As aggravating as you occasionally are, I would never make you eat a *turkey* dog, knowing your opinion of them."

"Bless you." He leaned forward and dropped a careless kiss on her cheek.

His warm, firm lips had barely left her skin, when they both froze.

Awareness crashed over her with the power of a stormy ocean. Her body reacted as if he'd dipped her over his arm and stolen the very breath from her.

Lynn was afraid to move, certain that even the slightest flinch would betray how he affected her.

He took forever to lean back away from her. When his eyes met hers, another layer of understanding darkened the blue of his eyes to almost sapphire.

A unique experience in her life.

On a gut level, she understood him, too, from what she knew of his history, what she had discovered about his parents. If only she could wrap her brain around it, she'd figure out how to proceed.

All because of turkey hot dogs.

He inclined his head toward the driver's seat of the rental car. "Get in and follow me. Dock's isn't far."

Unable to speak, her throat clogged with emotions she hadn't been bothered by in a good ten years, she nodded and climbed into the car.

He shut the car door tight, as if wanting to be assured of her safety, and strode to his motorcycle, which was parked right in front of her car.

She watched him pull his leather jacket on over his khaki uniform, his strong back and arms stretching and flexing. When he donned the gleaming black motorcycle helmet with its tinted visor, he ceased to be an officer and a gentleman; instead her imagination cast him in the role of mystery lover. Exciting. Dangerous.

Dangerous enough to be capable of a hit-and-run?

No. A thousand times no.

The roar of his bike's engine brought her mind back under her control.

She had to have learned something important to his case today. She *had* to have.

As she followed Rick through the base to the main gate open to the public, then into Oceanedge, she reviewed everything she'd overheard and seen.

Rick had held a newborn against his skin.

Rick had only ever made one mistake.

He'd do anything for his friends.

He was the best.

Lynn gritted her teeth and gripped the steering wheel. She *knew* all that. She knew it and she *believed* it.

What she didn't know were the whys.

She stilled as snippets of other conversations washed over her.

…but he didn't look so good, Rick.

She realized there was something else she didn't know.

The *who*.

A stone-solid, gut-level hunch formed. She'd bide her time with this one, though, until she had more information. So she didn't blow it.

She followed Rick down to the waterfront, where wharfs were built out into a small ocean inlet. He led her into the parking lot of a blue-and-white cottage-like restaurant at the end of its own little dock. So, its name was appropriate. And Dock's had small sailboats moored around it.

A lovely spot from which to watch the sunset.

A romantic spot.

Her heart started pounding again.

She slammed the gearshift into Park and yanked the keys out of the ignition. Why did her brain keep insisting on going there? She'd never had this sort of problem before. All her...*involvements* had served a purpose. None had anything directly to do with her work.

Certainly none had anything whatsoever to do with her heart.

As Lynn was pulling her small black purse from her briefcase, the car door opened. She turned to find a big, tan hand level with her nose, offering to help her climb out of the driver's seat.

The officer and gentleman was back.

She'd never had a problem remaining impartial before because she had never met a man like this before.

A man who understood her.

A man who tempted her.

Lynn slipped her hand into his, mesmerized by his

strong fingers closing slowly over hers. She pressed her clammy palm against the dry warmth of his. Her respiration became shallow when he helped balance her as she got out of the car. She could feel his gaze on her, but she avoided looking at him as she struggled for control.

Her body had never reacted to a man this way. Rick's combined emotional and physical impact on her—so powerful because it had been so unexpected—pried open the shell she'd always kept on her vulnerability. She would have to make a concerted effort to close herself up tight again.

No ties, no limits.

She stepped away to pretend to admire the restaurant, leaving him to shut the car door.

"Nice place," she offered.

"Yeah, it is." He slipped a hand to the small of her back and escorted her forward.

She'd become so accustomed to his touch in the past few days that she expected it. Wanted it. She scrambled for a rationalization.

Lack of sex. That had to be it. She hadn't been with a man for over two years. Not since she'd allowed herself to live a little at a conference with a fellow lawyer she'd known for years but saw rarely. They'd trusted each other enough to be sure the fling would be kept on the physical level. It had been, but despite the guy's good looks and skill as a lover, not satisfying enough to repeat.

Okay, now she had settled on a reason for her awareness of Rick. Time to deal with it.

Once inside the quaint, nautical-themed restaurant, they were seated at a table for two against the window that spanned the entire back of the room, similar to Rancho Margarita but without the heavily tinted glass.

Lynn gazed at the beautiful scene of sailboats, water and sky, and let out a calming breath. "How incredible."

"It is, isn't it," Rick agreed. "Growing up in the San Francisco Bay area, I've always had a thing for water."

She shifted her attention to his handsome profile. "Then it's a good thing Marines are amphibious."

He turned and grinned. "Yes, it is. And it's also one of the reasons I joined."

"Along with their tradition of honor."

His smile faded. "Yes." He waited for her to press more, his eyes wary, his jaw set.

She took a different tack. "Tell me about growing up in San Fran."

He blinked at her, then his face softened in surprise and, if she wasn't mistaken, pleasure. "Well, considering our present location…" He nodded at the small sailboats bobbing gently in their slips outside the window. "The most logical sea story to tell you is the one about me trying to learn to sail one of those things."

Rick spent the next half hour—through ordering their food and eating their salads—telling her how, at age ten, he'd not only managed to bonk into the Golden Gate Bridge's pilings, but was also capsized by a huge sea lion that had decided Rick's little training skiff would be a good sunning spot and had tried to climb aboard. He had her laughing so hard she had to cover her mouth with her napkin and struggle to keep from choking on a mouthful of lettuce.

After she could finally swallow, she said, "Oh, my gosh, that's hysterical."

"Today it is. At the time, I wasn't so sure. And my mother definitely didn't see the humor in it. That was pretty much the end of my sailing days."

Lynn sobered some. "She's very protective of you."

Rick shrugged. "I have guns for that, now."

His faint, mischievous grin coaxed her off the subject of his mother.

Their dinner arrived—shrimp scampi for Lynn and poached salmon for Rick—and conversation remained light. A lot of reminiscing for him, some deft evasion for her when the subject of her past came up.

She did, however, tell him some stories relating to her job—like the time a developer literally tried to sell McCoy Enterprises some swampland in Florida.

She set her fork on her empty plate, Rick's laughter filling her in a way the most satisfying meal never could. "He claimed to have assumed that, with the McCoys' billions, the family would be more than happy to pay to drain the land and have themselves some prime property. He didn't know that Alexander McCoy is as committed to conservation as his father is to the moral character of the community, and would never damage wetlands that way."

Rick frowned. "You mean his grandfather." It was clear by his tone that the idea of Marcus McCoy caring about the morality of anything was a little too much to swallow.

Realizing her slip, she sat back. "Yes. I mean his grandfather." She rubbed her temple. "I'm going to have to get that through my head before we go back to Dependable."

There was a long pause.

"I won't be going back to Missouri with you, Lynn." He wasn't arguing with her, just quietly stated the fact.

The waitress arrived with their bill. Lynn held her tongue until she was gone.

"You're wrong, Rick. Somehow—"

"The only place I'll be going anytime soon—" he pushed his chair back from the table and stood "—is for a walk on the dock. Care to join me?"

She hesitated, but decided arguing with him in the middle of a crowded restaurant wasn't in the best interests of either of them. Especially when he could simply walk out on her.

Besides, she should be lulling him into opening up to her, not putting him on the defensive.

"Yes, I would care to join you." She gathered her purse and stood while he counted out the money to pay their check and leave a tip.

She considered offering to put it on her expense-account credit card, but promptly dismissed the idea. It'd undoubtedly offend his sense of honor. If this were indeed a fantasy come to life, eventually he'd have to get used to her being the type of woman who preferred to pay her own way.

It wasn't, so there was no point.

After putting on his leather coat he offered her his elbow and escorted her out of the restaurant's back door, into the incredibly pleasant June evening.

The seagulls called and the water lapped against fiberglass hulls with a dull *thunk*. The salt tang to the air, hinted at while she'd been driving, was intense down here, coupled with the strong scent of kelp. Compared with some of the smells she remembered from her childhood, it was far from unpleasant. She filled her lungs and was simply reminded how alive she was.

Once past the empty outdoor eating area that must only be used for lunch service, they strolled to the end of the Dock's dock. A slight breeze they'd been sheltered from before carried away most of the ocean shore smell.

Lynn shuddered when the beauty, the serenity of the scene, sucked the tension from her.

"Cold?" Rick started shucking his jacket without waiting for her answer.

"No, not really." Although, before they'd gone into the restaurant she should have grabbed the suit coat that went over her dress. The fact that she hadn't felt cold in the air-conditioning proved how much he could distract her.

He swung his coat around her shoulders despite what she'd said.

She was instantly assaulted with the scent, warmth and weight of him. She'd never experienced anything so soothing, so protective, in her life.

Time to deal with it? *Yeah, right.* She wanted to float in this feeling forever.

He tugged the collar ends together under her chin and held on, an intimate move that made her gaze catch on his mouth.

She watched him say, "You love your job, don't you."

She nodded stupidly.

"Is that the reason you're so determined, or is there something else? Something to do with those pool halls you grew up in?"

She jerked her eyes to his as if he'd given her a shove into icy water instead of holding her close by the collar of his jacket. The speculation in his gaze held her beneath the surface until it seemed she had no air.

Her brain finally freed from the warm languor of her body and firing on all cylinders, she grasped at what little info she had and came up fighting. "Who's Pete?"

His expression shifted, became blank, then he raised his dark eyebrows a little too high. "Pete?"

Had she scored a hit? "Yes, Pete. I heard what you and Diane were saying, and I thought—"

"Do you know you have the most beautiful mouth I've ever seen?" His eyes glinted and he suddenly looked a little wild. But he sounded sincere.

Her heart stuttered. "What?"

"Your mouth. It's beautiful. Along with the rest of you." His head dipped toward her. "And very, very kissable."

"Are you insane—"

His mouth caught her accusation and her breath and pretty much all of *her* sanity, too.

The only thing left for her to do was kiss him back, but the yearning he'd stirred in her earlier leaked into the kiss.

And there wasn't a damn thing she could do about it.

Chapter Eleven

Even before he'd done it, Rick had realized kissing Lynn was a clichéd, hare-brained way to distract her from questioning him about Pete.

Heaven only knows why he'd done it anyway.

No. He knew damn well why. Because she *was* beautiful and kissable. But most important, because he believed in his gut she needed him to. She needed someone to show her she was worth holding on tight to.

Despite that being the very last thing he could offer her right now. Or ever.

What he really didn't know was why she was kissing him back with such soul-touching tenderness.

But their tongues found each other and he stopped caring why.

The force of the passion she ignited staggered him. He tightened his hold on the collar of his leather jacket around her neck in an attempt to anchor himself.

She moaned and leaned into him.

The weight of her pelvis against his sent a bolt of

electricity through his brain. Man, he wanted her. He wanted her in a way he'd never experienced.

With desperation.

He'd do anything, say anything, to have her.

Good God.

He broke off the kiss and stared down at her, breathing like he'd just finished the most grueling leg of the final phase of Marine basic training: the dreaded Crucible.

Her eyes were closed, her lush lips wet and parted, her breathing as erratic as his.

Because his life was no longer his own, he was becoming a desperate man. But he hadn't reached the place where he would put his own wants and needs before what he knew was right. He was *not* his father.

He eased away from Lynn.

She opened her eyes, blinking rapidly, clearly struggling for her equilibrium. The knowledge that the kiss had affected her as strongly as it had affected him, tested every ounce of discipline he had.

A weaker man would swoop down on her and claim her. He couldn't. She deserved better than to be a salve for the burn of his frustration and anger.

She wanted—deserved—something that couldn't be taken away.

He wasn't it.

"I'm sorry, Lynn," he croaked, his throat tight.

She put a hand briefly to her mouth, bewilderment flitting across her lovely flushed face, before she straightened her shoulders.

"No problem." She cleared her throat and looked away.

He should explain. *Oh, sure,* he silently scoffed at himself. Telling her he'd only kissed her to distract her from asking about Pete would really make it better.

Instead, he said, "We should probably go."

She couldn't contain her sarcasm. "Yeah. The people with window seats will probably think they'll have to pay extra for dinner *and* a show." She jerked her head toward the restaurant, where the low sun was glinting off the big windows running the entire length.

All he could think to say was "I'm sorry" again.

"It's okay. Really." She started walking back toward the restaurant.

Rick mentally ran through as many cuss words as he could think of as he followed her, which occupied him until they reached the back of the restaurant.

Instead of returning the way they'd come, through the outdoor dining area and inside, she went around the side of the building to the parking lot.

When she reached his motorcycle, she slipped his coat from her shoulders and laid it on the seat. "Thank you for this. And for dinner." She wouldn't look at him.

He was such a jerk. "Lynn—"

"I'll be in touch." She met his eyes only briefly before turning toward her rental car and digging the keys out of her small black purse.

"Lynn."

Her shoulders rose as she inhaled deeply. She faced him, her jaw set. "Whether it was your intent or not, you haven't chased me off, Rick. Sorry, but I'm not giving up."

His throat was so thick with regrets, all he could do was nod in acknowledgment.

She raised her chin, then turned back to the car door and unlocked it, opened it and climbed in.

He continued to stand there as she drove away, trying to come to grips with the fact he was glad she wasn't giving up.

LYNN DIDN'T SLEEP that night.

Instead she pored over the papers she had on Rick, spread across the white comforter of her hotel suite bed, and searched for any mention of a man named Pete in Rick's history.

Once she'd settled down enough, she realized Rick hadn't been trying to scare her off with his kiss; he'd been shutting her up. Stopping her from questioning him about this Pete guy after the name had popped into her head. She should know by now that Rick was the last person she should hope to get information from.

Unfortunately, the files she had were about as helpful. There was no mention of any Pete.

She thought about calling Ann Branigan again, but this Pete was apparently a mutual friend of Rick's, and Diane and Bill Stuttelford's. Talking to one of them made more sense. And she knew exactly where to find Major Stuttelford.

A workable plan in place, she finally drifted to sleep toward dawn.

The maid woke her up after two in the afternoon.

So much for catching Major Stuttelford first thing in the morning.

After asking the maid to come back later, Lynn showered, dressed in her last clean suit, a fitted red jacket with a matching skirt paired with a black semisheer blouse and black sling-back heels, and headed for the base.

While she risked running into Rick—she'd noticed the day before that Major Stuttelford's office was directly across from his—she needed to talk to the major in person. She'd met him only briefly, but he hadn't struck her as the type who'd be able to evade her questions without revealing something.

If he wasn't receptive to her at all, she could always express an interest in getting ahold of his wife to obtain a recipe or something from her. Maybe Diane would talk to her about Pete. She'd certainly sounded concerned about him.

When Lynn arrived at the building housing Weapons Training Battalion Command, she immediately spotted Rick's parked motorcycle.

Rats.

She parked as far away from the black-and-red motorbike as she could, but nowhere near the end window, which would belong to the colonel's office. Hopefully, that was where Rick would be working on the budget again.

Recreational Aquatics Thermal Regulator. Pul-lease.

She couldn't help but grin at how he'd suckered her with that whopper. To think she'd felt so bad for him.

Right there was the problem. She couldn't keep from feeling things for him.

Scary things.

She pushed her worries aside and slipped into the building. And was immediately noticed by Lieutenant Crane as he headed for the door. The red suit had been a bad call. The color shouted, *Check me out!*

Judging by the way his eyes flared when he got around to hers, he would have recognized her no matter what she'd worn.

He smiled broadly and extended his hand. "Lynn! Jay Crane, from the birthday party yesterday."

"I remember, Lieutenant."

"Sorry. It's just that we're used to looking alike to civis." He waved a hand at his uniform.

"Understood."

His eyes drifted to her legs. "I'm pretty sure Rick is in Colonel Bergstrom's office. At the end of the hall."

"Oh, okay. Thanks. Say—" She pretended the thought had just occurred to her, regaining his full attention. "Is Major Stuttelford in? I wanted to ask him for a recipe from Diane."

"Bill? No. I'm afraid not. He's out at the small-arms range to check in with the sergeants, which is where I'm heading. I can ask him to have Diane get ahold of you, if you'd like."

She shook her head as though it wasn't important. "That's okay. It can wait."

"All right. If you're sure." He started to move past her.

Lynn chewed on her lip for a moment, hating lost opportunities. So she took a risk. "Lieutenant?"

He stopped and glanced back at her.

She cocked her head. "Jay."

He smiled and stepped near again. Why wasn't Rick this easy to play? Because she wasn't attracted, both emotionally and physically, to this guy.

She mentally sighed at the conclusion and returned the lieutenant's smile, but made sure that hers was a little tenuous, as if she were worried. "Diane mentioned to Rick that she and Bill saw Pete, and his appearance worried them. Have you by any chance seen him?"

He frowned. "Pete?"

He thought about it long enough that Lynn started to fear her gut instinct was wrong.

"Pete Wright?"

She nodded in the hope she'd hit paydirt, her heart rate speeding up.

"No. I haven't seen him since he resigned his commission a few months ago. But I can't say I'm surprised if Diane said he looked bad." Jay shook his head in obvious disgust. "The guy was his own worst enemy. They didn't call him Pete *Wrong* for nothing."

Yes! Finally, something she could work with.

She struggled to hide her growing excitement. "Hmm. Well, that's too bad. But thanks anyway. I guess I better go find Rick."

"Sure." He raised a hand. "It was good seeing you again."

"Same." She waved goodbye, taking a few steps

toward the hall that led to the offices. As soon as he was out the door, she stopped.

She could keep going and see what reaction she'd get out of Rick by dropping the name Pete Wright, but Rick might not be as willing to confess in his CO's office what she was beginning to suspect was the truth. Plus, he might simply get up and leave rather than talk to her.

No, this called for an ambush at home, where he'd have to physically throw her out if he wanted her gone.

She'd claimed otherwise, but she had run away from him. Tonight, after he came home and had had a chance to unwind, she'd go see him—and not leave until she had the truth.

No matter what he said or did.

RICK DROPPED his head back onto his dark brown leather recliner and considered not opening the door. He knew who had knocked, had heard the tap of her high heels on the stairs as she'd climbed them. And he could tell by the way Buddy was swishing his tail as he watched out the window from his perch on the top of the couch.

She knocked harder, then punctuated her knocking by ringing the doorbell insistently.

She wouldn't go away. Even if she did, he wouldn't be able to stop thinking about her. He'd already tried enough to know it wouldn't work. Last night, the attempt had cost him what little sleep he might have gotten and soured his mood further.

His court date was fast approaching and all he could think about was kissing Miss Lynn Hayes.

Trying to rack it up to one more wicked twist of fate he had to accept, he pressed the off button on the TV remote, pushed himself out of his chair and went to answer the door.

He barely had it open before Lynn squirted through and stepped past him.

"Come on in," he offered more sarcastically than he'd intended.

But damn, why did she have to look so good in red? The vibrant color of her suit brought out the creaminess of her skin and made her hair look like black silk flowing over one shoulder. Her lipstick was a more subtle shade of red, but he still found himself fixating on her mouth like a gunner who couldn't leave the trigger alone.

He shook off the stupid comparison and closed the door.

She gripped her briefcase in front of her. "I saw Buddy jump off the couch and didn't want him to think he could get out."

Rick glanced down and saw that his cat was indeed curling himself around the entryway table leg, trying a little too hard to appear nonchalant.

Contrition took him down a notch. "Sorry. And thanks. I'm not exactly in the mood to have to chase him."

"You're welcome." She edged a little farther into the room. "But I'm not sure I'm going to improve your mood any."

He tried to appear surprised, and she smiled a little in response. She was clearly nervous, though, glancing away.

Dread belly-crawled through him.

She exhaled noisily and squared her shoulders. "I suppose I might as well just get to it." She went to the dining room table and set her briefcase on it. Facing him again, she rested her backside against the table and crossed her arms firmly beneath her suit-confined breasts.

All he could think of was setting them free.

"I know all about Pete Wright," she stated matter-of-factly.

Rick's knees loosened, forcing him to shift his weight and cross his own arms to keep his reaction from showing.

She held up a hand. "There's no point making up some story about why he looks the way he does. I have confirmation. But I'm very interested in hearing your side of all this before I do anything."

Rick mentally scrabbled for some out, but his brain wouldn't work. All he could come up with was "Confirmation?"

She sighed heavily. "Please, Rick. Tell me. Tell me why."

He forced his legs to work, to take him back to his recliner, where he plopped down. He'd known from the minute he'd laid eyes on her that she was smart, that she was going to cause him trouble. But he'd had no idea he would grow to care what she thought of him. He cared so much that his need for her to understand grabbed him by the throat and wouldn't let go.

He rested his elbows on his knees and stared at his limp hands. "Because I owe Pete my life."

"I knew it! I just knew it was something like that."

Great. She'd been on recon and he'd popped right up, waving with both arms like a big idiot.

She rushed over and dropped to her bare knees in front of him, fancy suit and all, so he'd have to acknowledge her. Those amber eyes of hers glowed fierce. "And now he wants you to throw it all away?"

"He doesn't see it that way." Pete would never get what this was costing Rick. The certainty was heartbreaking.

She caught one of his hands in hers, stroking the smooth pad of her thumb along his skin. It was all he could do not to grab her up in his arms and hold on tight. She would make some lucky man one hell of an anchor someday.

Too bad he was not a lucky man.

She said softly, "Start from the beginning, Rick. Please."

Her entreaty did him in. There wasn't much point in holding out when she already held the key piece to the puzzle in her hot little hand and would eventually fit it in place herself.

He pulled in a deep breath and let everything out. "Even though I hadn't seen him for a while, Pete called and asked to borrow my truck for the weekend. He said he had to pick up some furniture for the baby's room. I offered my help, but he said he didn't need it. So I let him have the truck. That night he showed up at my door, his face doing a great imitation of having said hello to a baseball bat."

"Or an airbag."

Rick nodded, clinging with surprising need to the small comfort of her hand on his. "He said he'd had a couple of beers too many and had crashed my truck into a tree. He'd said it wasn't all that bad, that the fact that he could still drive it back here was proof. Frankly, I was too angry to do more than glance over the railing at it.

"He begged me to tell the insurance company— or anyone else—that I'd been the one driving the truck. He'd lose his insurance if he was nailed for the accident, and without insurance he couldn't drive, and if he couldn't drive he'd lose his job, such as it is, and with the baby coming…" Rick ran his free hand over his face, a weariness like he'd never felt before settling deep in his bones.

She interjected, "So you agreed to claim responsibility." There was no judgment in her tone. Only understanding.

It meant the world to him.

"I've a clean record. At worst, I figured my insurance would go up, but with the new pay grade that had come with my promotion, any increase wouldn't be that big of a deal. But then the cops showed up, which surprised me. Still, when they asked if I'd been the one driving my truck about an hour earlier, I said yes. It was only then that I found out what had really happened, that Pete had hit another car, not a tree, and had fled the scene."

"But why not tell them the truth then?"

"Because the consequences for Pete would be even worse."

"So you decided to sacrifice yourself for him."

Rick stared into her beautiful, hurting eyes and gave the only explanation he could.

"I had no choice."

Chapter Twelve

Lynn glared at Rick, clenching and unclenching her teeth. So much for the elation of having been right about Rick's innocence. His reasoning was maddening.

He studied her in return. "You were bluffing when you said you knew everything about Pete Wright, weren't you?"

"Yes, I was," she admitted. "I'd overheard what Diane said to you about him, and something about your tone, your body language, everything, told me something was up."

"You have the most disconcerting way of seeing through me." He said it softly, without annoyance. With something like resignation.

Lynn's pulse raced and the yearning that had swamped her at the twins' birthday party returned to the pit of her stomach, until she ached as if she were starving.

His dark eyebrows slanted down suddenly. "But we never said his last name."

"Lieutenant Crane supplied that part." The words sounded strained, breathless.

"Jay? When?"

"Today. Just inside Weapons Training Battalion Command."

Reluctant admiration sparked in his eyes. "I didn't see you there."

"I know." His appreciation warmed her. Melted her. "After I had Pete's last name—and it took me a while to nail down the spelling—I spent the rest of the day making calls and searching the Internet for anything I could find out about him. But I really came up with only confirmation of his military service and an address."

She lowered her chin and reined in the warm fuzzies. "An address that led me to an apartment building just down the hill from your condo. Well within walking—or *staggering*—distance after dropping off a bashed-up truck. More than enough to convince me to confront you with the name."

"And trick me into spilling all."

Again, no condemnation, just the flat acceptance she'd noticed he sometimes exhibited when talking about his pending fate.

The one that pissed her off. "Yes. I had to trick you. It was the only option left open to me."

His face clouding, he shook his head. "Not the only option, Lynn. You could have done as I asked and gone back to Dependable."

"No. I couldn't."

"Because you want the promotion you'll get from hauling me back ASAP? The one that will give you the security you need?"

She looked away, shamed by the way he made her sound. Self-serving. Cold.

These things had never bothered her before; she'd actually embraced them out of self-preservation.

She added for him, "My third goal. Yes, security will always be part of what's motivating me here. But not all." She dared to meet his turbulent blue eyes again. "After I realized the type of man you were, there was no way I could walk away from what you've gotten yourself into."

"Why not?"

Decades worth of hurt and frustration exploded in her without warning. "Because no one should have to pay for something someone else has done. *Ever.* It's wrong and it messes people up for life. I should know." Tears formed in her eyes. Mortified, she stared at the ceiling and tried to blink them away.

One of his hands cupped her cheek. "What happened, Lynn?"

His gentle but strong touch and her desire to keep him from a similar fate brought the truth tumbling out. "My own parents framed me. I was working so hard—" Her voice broke. She cleared her throat of the anguish and pressed on. "So hard to get good grades in school so I could earn scholarships and get the hell away from them."

The humiliation she'd battled never to let out of its dark spot in her soul swamped her. "But they hid some stolen cash and crap they were trying to fence for a 'friend' in my room. And when the friend narced on them, they pointed the finger at me." She jabbed her own finger against her chest. Nothing could rival the pain of their betrayal.

"I was sent to juvie for a while and damn near got kicked out of school. Thank God they agreed to seal my records when I turned eighteen or I never would have been given the scholarships I needed or been accepted into law school." She shook her head and whispered, "Never."

"Oh, Lynn—" Empathy softened the stubborn line of his wonderful mouth.

She hated to be pitied, to be seen as vulnerable. Letting him in so deeply was like eviscerating herself in front of him. But she had to make him understand. "So you see? I know. I know from experience. They never cared. They never appreciated what I went through."

She shifted closer on her knees. "You can't do this, Rick. You can't take Pete's punishment. You have to go to the authorities and tell them the truth."

The stubbornness returned. "No, Lynn. I have to go through with it. Till the bitter end. Because Pete and I have some not-so-pleasant history of our own."

Rick took her hands and pulled her up with him as he stood. "I can't bear for you to be like this. Come here." He hugged her tight to him, but before she could sink into the potentially healing embrace, he let her go.

He led her over to the couch and sat down, urging her down next to him by not releasing her hands.

She complied. The physical connection felt so good. Almost too good to allow. She was still so afraid of being hurt.

Calling on her own stubbornness, she countered, "And I can't stand to watch you throw your life away."

He shushed her gently. "Give me a second and I'll tell you why it's for the best." He arranged their clasped hands on his thigh, his thumbs stroking hers the way she'd tried to soothe him. "Pete and I grew up together. We were best friends for as long as I can remember.

"We've always been very different, but I guess we initially gravitated toward each other because we each had only one parent at home. I had my mom, and he had his dad. Although, the only reason his mom wasn't around was that his dad had run her off. The guy drank too much and got ugly." The handsome lines of his face hardened with memories.

He looked down at their hands, traced his thumb along the creases of her knuckles. "Needless to say, Pete spent a lot of time at my house. But one day he showed up really beat to hell, and I decided it was time to get him out of there for good. So I snuck into his house and grabbed all his stuff for him. He'd been too scared to go back himself."

Lynn raised her eyebrows. "You didn't tell your mom?"

His mouth downturned, Rick gave a quick shake of his head. "Pete begged me not to. He didn't want his dad to go to jail. He just wanted away from him. Thank God his dad ultimately didn't care. Mom was pretty busy with work at the time, and bought our story that Pete had fallen out of a tree."

Having met savvy, protective Ann Branigan, Lynn had to ask, "She didn't suspect abuse?"

He shrugged. "She knew the guy was a loser, but he always put on a good show when he had to. Still, my mom was more than happy to help Pete get some distance from him."

"So he moved in with you."

"For a while. Until an aunt showed up and wanted him. She even moved to town so Pete could stay in the same school. I still watched over him as best I could, but the guy never seemed able to catch a break. If there was a screwup to be made, Pete Wright made it."

She remembered what Jay had said about him. "Earning him the nickname Pete Wrong."

He blinked at her. "That's right. That's what everyone called him. Even after we got him a scholarship and he joined the Marines with me, he could never make life work for him."

"So he drinks. Like his dad."

Rick shrugged again, his jaw tight.

"I'm sorry, Rick, but from the sound of it, Pete's the one who owes *you* a debt."

"No. I'd be dead if he hadn't pulled me out of a Humvee seconds before it took another hit from a hand-held rocket."

"In Afghanistan. Where you earned your Purple Heart."

He stared at her in surprise again.

"It's in your file, Branigan."

"Oh. Right. Of course."

"Okay, so he saved your life. I'd say you're even now."

"It's not that simple, Lynn. Pete needs me to be there for him again. He's got a baby coming—"

"Which he should have been thinking about, instead of tying one on and going for a joyride in your truck!" she interrupted, her anger resurfacing at the injustice of the whole situation. "Take it from me, a rotten childhood does not let you off the hook for the rest of your life. People have to own their behavior."

"Lynn, I made a commitment to Pete all those years ago. I have to honor it."

There was that word again. *Honor.* But it was the chaser of commitment that smoothed the bitter edges of the concept and made it easier for her to swallow. And once she got the whole thing down, it hit her hard.

Rick's blind devotion and stubborn honor touched her deeply. How different would her life have been if even one person had been that committed to her? Had been there for her. Had cared...

"Lynn?"

She jerked slightly, realizing she'd tightened her grip on his hands until her knuckles were white and his fingers were turning red. "Sorry."

She immediately released him and gave a short laugh, though it sounded strained to her ears. She searched for a plausible explanation. "I hate the fact that honoring your commitment to Pete will cost you everything."

He reclaimed her hands and nearly made her weep with his gentle strength and refusal to let her struggle alone. "I have less to lose than Pete."

She refused to let Rick condemn himself this way.

"No. I can't accept that argument. You have a life you love. Anyone with eyes can see that the Marines are your heart and soul. You can't just offer that up to Pete when you've already given him so much."

"I stopped having a choice the minute I told the police I was driving my truck that night."

"You always have a choice, Rick. There's always an alternative."

He locked gazes with her. "I wish there were this time, Lynn."

She opened her mouth to rail at him, to get him to accept reason. But suddenly she saw him, really processed what she'd had glimpses of the first time they'd spoken of this.

Helplessness had gouged dark circles under his amazing blue eyes, eyes that were clouded by despair. Deep grooves bracketed his mouth, as if he'd kept his lips sealed too tight for too long.

She really wanted to cry now. The only way to stave off the waterworks was to be strong for him, to truly comfort him if she could. For once, he deserved to be on the receiving end, rather than always on the giving end.

And there was only one way she knew how.

"Oh, Rick," she murmured, revealing the pain she felt for him. She leaned forward and captured his lips tenderly with hers.

He stayed perfectly still for a moment, probably warring with his overblown sense of what was right and wrong. Or worse, wondering if she was trying to manipulate him somehow.

With her lips she tried to show him how much she hurt for him, how much she cared. That she only wanted to make things better, at least for a short time.

Just when she feared her coaxing wasn't working, that he didn't want this with her, his mouth opened and he kissed her back with the same passion he'd built to on the dock. He released her hands and brought his up to her face, holding her so he could deepen the kiss.

She could taste his desperation, and set out to encourage him to give her every last drop of it. She had far more experience dealing with anguish than he did, had used it for years to fuel her struggle to achieve as much as she could as fast as she could.

Burying her hands in his short, thick black hair, she arched into him, then used her weight to draw him backward with her on the couch.

And squashed the cat.

Buddy didn't scramble to get out from under her or panic in any discernible way, but he did let out the most piteous, mournful yowl she'd ever heard.

Lynn jerked upward and broke off the kiss. "Buddy!" But the cat wouldn't move, even though she knew he could. And dang well should.

Rick made a grumbling noise and released her as he sat up, looking around her to the cause of the interruption. "That cat would rather be flattened than give an inch."

Figuring the moment to form a healing connection for them both was ruined, Lynn joked, "Hmm. Interesting character trait."

Rick smirked at the jab that would apply to all of them. "Well, in this instance—" he pushed himself off the couch and turned to her "—I choose life." He held his hands out to her. "If you're interested, I'd very much like you to join me."

She wrinkled her forehead in question while automatically slipping her hands into his. She didn't care what he meant as long as he continued to want to touch her. As long as he continued to let her soothe him.

He pulled her to her feet, his strength obvious in his deliberateness. "That is, assuming I'm reading you right."

Anticipation set her heart racing again. She came up against all that hardness and grinned. Wrapping her arms around his neck, she nodded. "Yes." She rubbed her hips against his. "You are most *definitely* reading me right."

He growled, "Hoo-rah," and picked her up. After carrying her into his bedroom, he used his heel on the door to shut Buddy out.

HE'D LOST HIS MIND.

That was the only explanation for why he'd carried Lynn into his bedroom. The parking-lot lights shining in through his open blinds on the single large window provided modern-day mood lighting and made his king-size bed on the far wall easy to find. Although, he still wasn't sure how far they'd take things. Lynn touched her tongue against his as she kicked her high heels off, and Rick decided he didn't care.

Both had been very clear about not wanting a relationship, and she'd left no doubt that she could separate the physical from the emotional. So they were indulging in a little sexual comfort. He was okay with that.

For a few hours, he selfishly would allow himself to take what was being given him.

And what a gift…

He laid her on his bed and stood gazing down at her, the thin strips of light falling on her as romantically as candlelight. Her long black hair pooled around her head on his beige comforter, begging for his fingers. Her open red jacket revealed a black blouse that hinted at the black lace beneath, and her red skirt rode up her toned thighs.

She looked like an ad for a sexy movie. One he'd want to watch over and over again.

In awe, he said, "Do you have any idea how beautiful you are?"

She raised her arms. "Come here and show me."

He bit his tongue to keep from *yes, ma'am*-ing her, and bent to pull off his shoes. He started to climb onto the bed next to her, but she stopped him with a raised hand.

She pointed at the colored bars pinned over his heart. "All those metals might poke me. Why don't you lose the shirt."

"The same could be said about the buttons on your shirt *and* jacket."

She smiled slow and sensually. "True." She started to sit up, reaching for her lapels.

"No. Let me." His fingers flew over his buttons, his focus on the tiny black ones on her blouse.

"Sir—yes, sir," she all but purred, and relaxed back down.

He grinned and whipped off his shirt, then climbed onto the bed with every intention of lying next to her to make it easier to peel her jacket and blouse off. But when he got close enough to smell her, his body automatically settled directly on top of her. Man, he was hard for her, and couldn't keep from fitting himself against her.

Her gasp echoed his response to the explosion of fiery sensation rippling through him from the contact and he started kissing her again.

She gripped his arms, right where the Marine insignia tattoo rode his biceps.

She tasted as exotic and tempting as she smelled and the feel of her beneath him made him burn. There was suddenly no doubt about how far they would take this.

If she wanted it.

Lynn rocked his world on so many levels. The passion in her kisses, growing more feverish by the minute, matched his, and she had a battle-honed inner strength he could lean on for a little while.

Just a little while.

She brought her arms up beneath his and wrapped them around him, the sleeves of her red suit coat deliciously rough against his bare sides. Skimming her hands down his back, she traced his muscles with her smooth fingertips as if mapping him. He ached for her to grab on tight and pull him into her.

The thought alone was enough to make him moan in the back of his throat.

When she encountered the thick ridge of one of his scars, she felt along it, then eased her mouth from his. "From the attack on your Humvee?"

Breathing heavily with the need to make love to her, he struggled to answer. "Yeah." An unpleasant thought occurred to him. "I hope they don't turn you off, because there's a bigger one on my hip."

She kissed him lightly. "No, not at all. They're a part of who you are. They make me proud of you. And humble me."

He stroked her silky hair back from her exquisite face. "Stop. The kinds of wounds I suffered are easy to deal with." Not to mention less damaging emotionally. She was the one with scars. Ones far too deep to touch.

The urge to try seized him.

Rick tipped his weight to the side and began unbuttoning her blouse.

"Shouldn't we take my jacket off first?"

"I'll peel them off together. A good Marine never wastes time or effort."

She brought a hand up and caressed the side of his face, reminding him he was no longer a good Marine. Despite the mostly unspoken support he'd received from his superiors, he might soon not be *any* kind of Marine.

Pain ripped through him and he sought solace, distraction, anything, in her kiss.

He found a mind-numbing heaven.

Lynn answered his sudden desperation in kind, popping open the front clasp on her lacy black bra before he'd freed the last button on her blouse. She yanked one side of her bra, blouse and jacket off in one motion. Damn, she was his kind of girl. He took care of the other side.

Rick paused long enough to drink in the sight of her bare breasts, creamy and full. As perfectly suited to his tastes as the rest of her.

He was about to say as much, but she distracted him by reaching to undo the side zipper of her skirt at the same time that she recaptured his mouth with hers. When she lifted her hips, he helped her push the snug garment off. Intentionally or not, her panties went with it.

He had to touch her, taste her. All of her. The way she moved beneath his hand, arched toward him, made blood roar in his ears.

Before long she yanked her mouth from his and begged, "Make love to me, Rick. Please."

Empowered for the first time in weeks, he instantly rolled toward the nightstand and snatched open the top drawer. "I want you so bad, Lynn," he murmured as he dug out a condom, always on hand regardless of his relationship status. Another way he refused to be like his father.

When he looked back into Lynn's face while he stripped off the rest of his clothes and chucked them aside, her soft smile expressed her understanding. After such a short time, she knew him so well.

The certainty stirred something powerful in his

chest that he wasn't inclined to examine at the moment. But he couldn't keep it from showing. He couldn't mask the impact she had on him.

He simply accepted that the woman stirred him, period.

Minutes later they found a crashing release together, made more volatile, more satisfying, by the intense emotions of the past few weeks.

As he collapsed onto his side, pulling her with him, a faint voice in his head reminded him that the yearning he'd seen in her golden-brown eyes and felt in her kiss was not something to be taken for granted. He needed to handle her with care.

He wouldn't dream of doing otherwise.

Not because she'd punch his lights out—or more likely, sue his ass—if she felt he'd done her wrong in a personal way. But because Rick was forced to admit the part of him stirred the most was his heart.

And that it would never be the same.

Chapter Thirteen

The bright morning sunlight streaming through Rick's bedroom window woke Lynn, but it was an inner glow that warmed her. Contentment—that was what it was. Bone-deep contentment. A new, foreign feeling.

She liked it.

The sensation stemmed from more than mind-numbing physical gratification. Something had happened between them last night. Something had taken root. A space she'd had before, an emptiness, had been filled. She'd swear on her career that the same had happened with him. It'd been there in his eyes, his touch.

Surely now, Rick would be willing to change his mind about letting her help him. The way he'd held her in the night, the trust, the connection she felt with him—these had to be enough to sway him. She knew it in her gut the same way she'd known his innocence.

Her limbs languid, she stretched as she rolled from her side onto her back. Looking to the pillow next to her, she simultaneously registered that the

shower in the adjacent master bath was running and
that a cat was staring at her. Rick was already up and
Buddy had commandeered his pillow.

Ick.

She met the cat's flat, unblinking blue gaze, so *not*
like his master's, which had been full of soul-touching need and body-tingling desire.

"Look here, cat. I let you have the couch, but I'm
claiming this bed as *mine*." She surprised herself by
meaning it. "At least until your daddy and I return to
Dependable. Then he'll be in *my* bed." The thought
tickled her to no end, permeating her with a buzzing
energy that was hard to contain. "I might even be inclined to let you come with us. I could use your carrier as a footrest on the plane. How does that sound,
Buddy?"

The cat stunned her by leaning forward to rub his
cheek on the top of her head, purring loudly like a
rusty chainsaw.

She laughed and reached up to pet him. "Keep that
up and I might have to reevaluate my opinion of cute
and fuzzy."

"Which is?"

Lynn started. Raising her head, she found Rick
standing in the bathroom doorway, a shoulder
propped casually against the door frame and a navy
blue towel draped low on his lean hips.

Oh, my.

His tanned shoulders and chest, their muscles
clearly defined, glistened here and there with moisture. He'd missed a dollop of shaving cream on his

throat. Right where she'd run her tongue at around one a.m. this morning.

Her skin tightened as she remembered what he'd felt like against her, how the dark hair on those long, strong legs had tantalized her skin as his legs tangled with hers.

She sighed in satisfaction and arched ever so slightly on the bed. "Not nearly as high as my opinion of hot and hard."

A dark eyebrow twitched upward. "Is that so?"

She pushed onto her elbows, not overly concerned whether the sheet covering her bare, hard-tipped breasts stayed put. "Affirmative." She gave a quick lift of her chin. "You missed a spot wiping off your shaving cream. Come here, and I'll use that towel of yours to get it."

He grinned and sauntered toward her. "I bet you will."

She made a grand show of nodding sagely. "And you never know where else you might have missed some of it."

"Shaving cream can be evasive stuff." His eyes were hot on her, but he stayed out of her reach.

"Maybe you should show me just how evasive…" she hinted. Despite having made love with him three times during the night, Lynn hadn't had enough of this man.

She might never get enough.

The thought was at once scary and thrilling. No way could she analyze what her need meant to her *no ties, no limits* lifestyle, with him standing before her in nothing but a towel and a tattoo.

He sucked air through his teeth. "Tempting, woman, very tempting." He sighed and looked out the window, shaking his head slowly. "But it's already pretty late—"

"Oh, right!" She snatched the sheet to her chest and popped to her knees on the bed. "We should try to get in to see the DA as early as possible to start the paperwork for having the charges against you dropped. We probably won't be able to dodge obstruction of justice, but that shouldn't bring more than a fine, some community service and maybe probation, and I can finagle around that."

Rick quickly sat on the side of the bed next to her. "Lynn—"

She was energized with purpose and hope, and her brain clicked furiously. "Considering what you'll be going for, we shouldn't have any trouble obtaining permission for you to leave the state."

He took hold of her upper arms and captured her gaze with his earnest, worried, determined eyes. "Lynn. Sweetheart. We're not going to the DA." He ran his thumbs up and down the sensitive skin on the underside of her arms, but that wasn't what raised goose bumps. "Nothing has changed. I'm not recanting my initial statement."

Feeling as if she'd been dropped off a cliff into a big fat, cold nothing, Lynn stared at him. "What do you mean you're not recanting your statement? That nothing's changed. I thought…I mean…" She was floundering.

Oh, no. While he hadn't misread *her* last night, she

sure as heck had misread *him*. She pulled away. Physically and emotionally.

His gaze was fierce. He probably thought his frustration matched hers.

He had no idea.

She held his gaze despite the bitterness eating away at her heart like acid. She'd allowed the fantasy to go too far, to sink beneath her skin.

In his eyes she could see he was stubbornly clinging to his extreme definition of honor.

At least when it came to his friend Pete.

Her resentment could only be trumped by her anger at herself for believing she had the power to heal him. And worse, for allowing him to penetrate the shell around her heart that she'd spent decades building. The fact that he had waltzed in so easily, so *quickly,* scared her.

But God, he'd been worth the risk.

Lynn scooted over to the opposite side of the bed and swung her feet to the floor. Rick had the sheet pinned beneath him, and didn't budge when she yanked on it, so she stood up naked.

He'd already unwittingly stripped her of all her protection, all her armor. She might as well make it literal. Her skin prickled both from the cold, now that she was no longer in his warm bed, and from the weight of his stare as she walked around the bed, collecting her clothing, before moving away from him to the bathroom.

"Lynn, honey—"

She closed the bathroom door behind her.

Nothing could strip her of her stubbornness. Or her determination. She refused to give up.

She would not, could not, let Rick sacrifice everything dear to him.

Nor would she leave this town without redeeming herself. It was the only way she'd regain her self-respect.

LYNN PULLED her rental car into a parking space next to one of the three Dumpsters directly across from 27A.

Pete Wright's apartment.

The orange-red Pontiac Firebird registered to him was parked in a space directly in front of the door, so he was probably home.

She'd already driven past it once this morning, on her way back to her hotel from Rick's, and the temptation to stop then and wring the guy's neck had been huge. Only, that wasn't how she wanted to make Rick's supposed friend pay for what he'd done, as appealing as the thought of waking him up to jump on his head was.

Especially after Rick hadn't tried to stop her from leaving.

So she'd forced herself to keep going, her window partially down so the breeze would help wake her up; she hadn't wanted to take the time to stop for a coffee. It would have had to be a triple shot of espresso after the night she'd had…embarking on more than one trip to her new definition of paradise.

She'd gone back to the hotel room she hadn't slept in the night before and had changed out of the clothes she'd worn yesterday. After showering, she'd put on the lone pair of blue jeans she'd brought with her on this trip, a plain white T-shirt and her running shoes. She'd dug her penlike, voice-activated, digital audio recorder out of her briefcase, had snagged her purse and had driven the couple of miles back to the Paradise View Apartments.

Lynn glanced at the Dumpsters, their lids propped open by a busted kitchen chair, the smashed box for a big-screen TV she doubted anyone living here could really afford and the expected black and white trash bags.

She smirked humorlessly. Some view. She was even less convinced that Pete had more to lose than Rick.

Her jaw set, she grabbed her recorder from where she'd stuck it in the center-console drink holder and her purse off the passenger seat. She made sure the recorder worked, then tucked it in an outer pocket on her purse but left it sticking out far enough for the microphone to be effective.

The sound of an apartment door shutting reached her through the open car window. She glanced up at the rearview mirror. A pregnant woman in maternity business clothes had come out of 27A and was going to an older white Subaru parked in the space next to the Firebird.

Rick's words came back to her: *He's got a baby coming.*

Must be Mrs. Wright. She was pretty—sweet-looking. She should be in a comfy chair with her feet up, instead of going to work, as she apparently was doing.

How many times had Pete gotten it wrong with her?

In the rearview mirror Lynn watched the woman unlock and open the driver's door on the Subaru and maneuver her cumbersome shape behind the wheel.

Lynn's dislike for Pete festered. Not only was he sending his very, *very* pregnant wife to work, but he hadn't even come out to help her into the car, let alone see her off.

The jerk.

The door to the apartment opened and a tall, skinny guy burst out with bed-mussed dark brown hair. He was wearing a stretched-out lime-green T-shirt that had seen better days and long, loose gray gym shorts. His big, white feet bare, he gingerly made his way to the Subaru.

Hello, Mr. Wright, destroyer of other people's lives.

He sported what looked to be a thick scab across the bridge of his nose and yellowish fading bruises under both eyes. *Airbag,* she thought.

Lynn wished she could say she was surprised by Pete in the flesh, but he was exactly as she'd pictured him. Scrawny. Unkempt. *A loser.*

A lot like her dad.

Her lip curled automatically. Since upsetting pregnant women wasn't her thing, and it wouldn't serve her purpose to confront him with his wife around—satisfying though it might be to make him squirm—Lynn waited and watched.

Pete dodged the open driver's door and bent to hand something to his wife. A red insulated lunch bag.

He said loud enough for Lynn to hear, "Thought

you could sneak out without this, didn't ya? Well, I don't care how fat you feel. Both of you need to eat. I made you a turkey-and-cheese sandwich on sourdough, and sliced up a couple apples that you can munch on during breaks. Okay?"

"Yes, Mother," his wife complained, but Lynn could see her smile reflected in the Subaru's side mirror.

"Just promise me you'll eat."

"I will. And thank you, sweetie."

He shrugged expansively. "It's the least I can do." He pulled the shoulder strap on the seat buckle out for her so she wouldn't have to twist to reach for it, and helped buckle her in. Once his wife was settled, he shut the door for her and backed up with a wave goodbye.

Lynn scowled and worked her jaw back and forth. Okay, maybe not a total jerk. And maybe she did see where Rick was coming from. A little.

Didn't matter. What Pete—and his wife—stood to lose didn't change the fact that Pete, not Rick, should be paying for his drunk driving and the accident he caused. One innocent person had been punished already by simply being in his way. There was no reason Rick should have to join the driver of the other car as one of Pete's victims.

His wife and unborn child were unfortunate but unavoidable collateral damage in his destructive behavior.

Lynn waited until Pete's wife had driven away before getting out of her rental car, by which time Pete had gone back into his apartment. Recorderoutfitted purse hanging high beneath her arm from its short handles slung over her shoulder, she walked to his door and rang the bell.

The door opened and Lynn found herself staring right at the remnants of a monster bruise on Pete's upper chest before he pulled his T-shirt back down. Airbag again. She also noticed the silver beer can in his hand. It might be after five p.m. somewhere in the world, but it didn't change the fact that he was having beer for breakfast.

At her raised eyebrows he said, "You just caught me about ready to get into the shower." He hoisted the can. "Shower pop." Then he looked at her. Really *looked* at her. He hitched an arm high on the door, planted his other hand on his hip and cocked a knee. "*Hi*. What can I do for *you?*"

At some point in his life he must have decided a heavy-lidded gaze and a half smirk were sexy. In fact, they made him appear either stoned or stupid. If she hadn't just seen him interacting with his wife, Lynn would have assumed he was both.

His personality-points total spiraled back downward. He might be solicitous to his expectant wife, but he was still slimy. She hid the fact that he left a bad taste in her mouth by smiling and offering her hand.

"Pete Wright?"

He nodded and squeezed her hand a little too tightly. "Yep, that's me!"

"Hi, Pete. I'm a friend of Rick's."

Pete straightened and the wolfish expression fell away. "Oh." His handshake was perfunctory.

Despite the disgust churning in her stomach, she hung on to his hand when he would have let go. Shifting her weight and arching her back slightly, she dropped her chin to regard him from beneath her lashes—a look she *knew* was sexy on her. "*Just* friends." She gave his hand one last suggestive squeeze before she let go.

The biologically rooted spark of male interest back in his light blue eyes, he opened the door wider and stepped aside. "Well, in that case, come right in." He gestured Lynn into the small but tidy apartment, brightened only by the natural light shining through a sliding glass window in the eating nook across the way.

The cramped living room was furnished with obviously inexpensive but not unattractive pieces. A brownish blue couch, a dark blue recliner, and wooden rocking chair and footrest with sky-blue pads arranged around an entertainment unit sporting—oh, yes—a big-screen TV. So things weren't all wrong for the Wrights. Or, more likely, for their credit-card company.

Pete closed the front door. "But I have to warn you, I'm a happily married man."

Too little, too late. She faced him. "I'm glad, because I'm here to help Rick take the fall for you."

His smarmy smile faltered, shifting into something ugly. "Wonder Boy doesn't normally need help. With anything."

Lynn schooled her features, even though she would have tossed her breakfast if she'd had any. To think Rick believed he owed this man something. "Well, it seems the authorities are having a hard time swallowing his version of what went down that night."

"Then he's not telling it very well, because I laid out for him what happened. At least, what I could remember."

Lynn dug her nails into her palm to keep from popping Old Petey a good one right between the eyes. The bastard. He'd nearly killed a woman that night. No kind of nightmare childhood or amount of emotional baggage could justify that kind of behavior. She'd managed to rise above hers, as hope sucking as it'd been; so could he. If he chose to.

She laughed, praying it sounded real. "Good. Then why don't you do the same for me, so I can back Rick up. Maybe I could say I was at Rancho Margarita with him, then saw him drive off and hit that other car."

Pete tucked his hands beneath his shirt, stretching it out further. "It's a shame you didn't see it." He shook his head in obvious amazement. "Man, did I ever clock that Volvo." He pulled his hands out and drove a fist into the palm of his other hand. "Bam! Spun the thing right around. Those are seriously well-built cars."

He touched a couple of fingers to the bridge of his nose. "If it hadn't been for the damn airbag in Mr. Safety First's rig, it would have been totally cool. Especially when I found out the other driver wasn't all that hurt."

Lynn cocked her head at him. "You don't think the other driver was injured?" Why wouldn't Rick have told him?

Pete gave a dismissive wave. "Oh, I know she got busted up a little. I checked on her before I drove off, to make sure she wasn't dying or anything. But that just means she'll score more from the insurance company. Hell, I'd let someone break my pelvis if I knew it would land me a settlement that would set me up sweet for life."

"How did you find out she had a broken pelvis?"

He shrugged. "Rick must have told me."

She felt a small measure of relief that Rick had at least attempted to convey how destructive Pete's actions had been. "So you didn't try to find out more for yourself later?"

"Why should I? Wonder Boy has it handled."

There was such derision in his use of the nickname. Lynn wondered if Rick was aware of how Pete really felt about him. Or maybe this snideness was something new. Stemming from guilt…?

Either way, Rick needed to hear this so he'd see how misplaced his loyalty was.

Lynn shifted her purse forward slightly to be certain the microphone on the pen recorder would work. "Speaking of 'Wonder Boy' having this handled, why don't you tell me everything you did that night—everything you can remember—" she winked at him and smiled as if she also thought destroying people's lives was one big joke "—so I can back Rick up."

Pete obliged, his confession more than once bordering on boasting. For the second time she found herself grateful that she hadn't had any breakfast, because she definitely would have yakked on the guy's skinny bare feet. Rick was sadly mistaken thinking he could save Pete from himself.

The only person who needed saving in this situation was Rick.

"I'M NOT IN THE MOOD for this, Buddy," Rick growled as he reached through the stairs in an attempt to grab ahold of his cat without getting his uniform filthy.

Unimpressed, Buddy darted out from under the stairs.

Right to the running-shoe clad feet of a beautiful woman Rick had thought couldn't get any more beautiful. But seeing her dressed down in snug jeans and a T-shirt, with her long black hair free around her shoulders, took his breath away.

He also would have sworn Lynn couldn't be any more dangerous to him than she already was. She understood him, saw right through the lies and believed in him enough to fight him. But when she looked like she could so easily be a part of his world, he was struck by how badly he wanted her to be. Suddenly, his career—which ironically he would soon be without—wasn't enough.

The fact that she had not only come back, but had come back dressed as though she intended to stay, made his heart pound. Hope stirred.

He shut it down. They could have no future because *he* had no future.

She bent and picked up Buddy, who started purring so loud he could be heard a couple of yards away. "He didn't slip out when I left earlier this morning, did he?"

Rick straightened, trying to rein in his equally erratic physical—and damn it—emotional response to her. "No. I wasn't paying as much attention as I should have when I was leaving for work." He gestured to where he'd dumped his motorcycle helmet and leather jacket on the landing when he'd realized he had a feline escapee.

She nodded and snuggled the cat, who snuggled her right back.

His heart ached at the sight. As he walked toward her, Rick said, "So you have reevaluated your opinion of cute and fuzzy?"

She heaved a sigh and stared him in the eye. "I'm fighting it."

"At least you're honest." And funny and wonderful and brave and unlike anyone he'd known before...

"Speaking of honest..." She handed Buddy to him and reached into a pocket of her purse, which was slung over her shoulder. "I have something I want you to hear." She held up what appeared to be a thick silver pen, but the grid pattern on the top gave it away as a voice recorder. "And it can't wait."

She marched past him and grabbed his helmet and jacket—probably so he couldn't just leave—then headed up the stairs to his condo.

Foreboding slowed his heart rate and brought his senses to battle-ready. He tucked Buddy, who had the sense not to squirm, under his arm and followed her.

Rick had locked the door, having not noticed right off that the cat had slipped by him, so Lynn had to wait for him to let her in. If he hadn't needed to put Buddy inside, he would have refused her. He was sure he wasn't going to like what she had to share with him.

His attention snagged on the mouth he'd spent hours worshiping last night, and he was forced to call himself a liar. He would let Lynn in anywhere. Maybe even into his heart.

The startling thought closed his throat up tight and made breathing difficult.

Time to lay on the breaks, anyhow.

Her life was in Dependable. His was here. In jail, then on probation. Far too similar to what she'd dedicated her life to getting away from. He wouldn't tempt her to fail.

He unlocked the door and opened it for her.

"Thanks," she said a little breathily, and went inside.

Maybe he wasn't the only one thinking about last night. But the way she'd left with barely a word of goodbye, he doubted she was planning a repeat performance. Although, he'd been wrong about her before.

His blood started rushing around and added to the chaos going on inside him, so he came only far enough into the condo to shut the door behind himself. He put the cat down, crossed his arms over his chest and looked pointedly at the recorder. "What have you got there?"

"Pete's confession," she stated baldly, as though she was telling him it was supposed to be partly cloudy that day.

Rick's world tilted and he practically staggered forward a step. "What?"

She held up a hand. "Just listen." She hit a button on the recorder with her manicured thumbnail, and he had no choice but to hear her visit with Pete, from his practically hitting on her "hello" to his "Rick better not screw this up" goodbye.

Pete's words nailed him in the chest with the accuracy of a smart bomb, obliterating him.

Rick planted a hand on the entryway wall and asked, "Do you plan on helping me by backing up my story?"

She gave him a stone-cold glare. "You're joking, right? Weren't you listening? Didn't you hear how hateful he was? You can't honestly tell me you're still planning to give up everything you've earned, everything that's dear to you, for this guy. He's not worth scraping off your combat boots, Rick!"

She paced across the dining room and back. "I would have killed to have someone like you in my life. No way in hell would I talk about you the way he does."

Something in his chest convulsed at her admission, but he fought it.

She shook her head vehemently, sending strands of sleek black hair flying. "I will *not* be backing your story up. If anything, I'll be playing this recording for the DA."

She might as well have shot him in the chest. "No, you won't."

She fisted her hand around the recorder as if suspicious he'd try to wrest it from her. He considered doing just that, but knew she'd fight him. Plus, once he touched her, he'd have a hell of a time letting her go. He was such a fool…

With enough bravado for an entire battalion, she declared, "If you won't admit you're lying for that sad sack, yes, I will."

He pushed off from the wall and prowled closer to her. "Pete didn't know you were recording your conversation with him, did he?" Purposefully, he crowded her. The memories of last night were too fresh and he wasn't as strong around her as he should be.

She widened her stance, seemingly unafraid of him. "Of course not."

"Then I'm positive you won't take that illegally obtained confession to the DA. You'd never risk your career that way."

"The recording could always show up at the district attorney's office anonymously. In case you didn't notice, I never identified myself to Pete, but he confirmed who he was quite plainly."

Rick's chest throbbed with a hurt that made his shrapnel wounds seem like mere scratches. He had thought she understood him. The disappointment was crushing.

He lashed out. "You really have no honor whatsoever, do you? Why can't you see I don't have a choice?"

Surprisingly, her eyes filled with tears.

His chest didn't just throb anymore; it felt ripped wide open.

Despite the blow he'd obviously dealt her, she lifted her chin. "There's no honor in enabling, either, Rick. And as long as you're still breathing, you *always* have a choice."

She leveled a finger at him. "You claim to be committed to Pete, but he'll never get the help he so plainly needs this way." She dropped her hand in disgust and moved away from him. "Do you know he was already drinking when I went to see him this morning?"

The bottom fell out of his stomach. "Was Marissa there?"

"His wife?" At his nod she shook her head and wiped at her reddening nose. "I waited until she left for work before knocking on his door. They struck me as having something that's worth trying to save, too."

The *too* caught at him, made him bleed. He ignored the ache for what might have been between them. "That's what I'm trying to do."

"No!" She actually stomped her running-shoe-clad foot. "You're just postponing the inevitable. Something worse will happen, Rick. Maybe to Marissa and the baby."

Calling on every speck of grit in him, Rick shook his head. He couldn't go there, couldn't bear the thought. The guilt alone would put him under.

"It's only a matter of time, Rick, and you know it. What about the woman he already hurt? What about

Emelie Dawson?" Lynn held up the recorder again. "He doesn't feel any remorse. You heard him. He thinks the insurance settlement she'll get from *your insurance company* makes it okay. Maybe you should go ask her if the money makes what she's going through okay. If a fat payday takes away the physical torment and the knowledge her life might never be the same."

A tear finally breached the rim of Lynn's thick lashes and slid down her smooth cheek. "Are you brave enough to do that? Are you brave enough to see for yourself the damage your friend is capable of? If you are, then while you're there, ask yourself how you'll feel the next time he drives drunk and someone else pays the price."

More tears followed, and he could tell she'd come to the end of her emotional rope.

His own rope rapidly fraying and his throat closed tight, he reached for her, but she held up a staying hand and marched past him.

"We've all got to do what we've got to do, Rick. And what I have to do is back in Missouri." She opened the door. "Good luck with what you've been doing here." Then she was gone.

Rick stared at the closed door. He had never felt emptier in all his life.

Or less honorable.

Chapter Fourteen

Berating herself every way she knew how for letting Major Rick Branigan sneak past her emotional defenses, Lynn slammed shut the driver's door on her rental car. At the same moment her cell phone beeped in her purse to let her know a text message waited for her on her phone.

She dug out the phone and accessed the message.

It was from Joseph McCoy himself.

Lynn's palms automatically grew damp.

She read it, and her stomach lurched. Though Joseph intended to give her the credit despite her lack of success, he had arranged for a plea bargain, in which Rick would plead "no contest" to a lesser charge, pay a fine and immediately be released from obligation if he agreed to come to Dependable, Missouri.

For good.

Lynn tossed her phone onto the passenger seat. Obviously, there wasn't a Marine base in Dependable, so Rick would have to be discharged. Dishonorably. Because even though he wouldn't be admitting his innocence or guilt, but rather not contesting the charges against him, it still meant a conviction.

Oh, how he'd hate that. Almost as much as he'd hate *her* if she took Pete's confession to the authorities.

With the deal Joseph had finagled, Rick would have to leave for Dependable. Exonerating him would free him of more than just his legal problems. He would refuse to see her for going against him.

She started crying in earnest—something she hadn't done in a very long time. She didn't want Rick to hate her.

But more, she didn't want him to be thought guilty of something he didn't do. Even if it cost her the promotion. Or Rick.

She squared her shoulders, started the car and left Rick's condominium complex. Although going to the district attorney and playing Pete's confession for him would very likely cost Lynn her job at McCoys because of the possible negative, scandalous publicity, as well as potentially get her disbarred, she had to do it. Illegally obtained or not, the recording would clear Rick of all but blind loyalty to a former friend.

Her jeans and T-shirt raised a few eyebrows and significantly delayed her getting in to see the DA, Robert Cummings, but once his assistant heard the evidence she had to present, he rushed her to his boss before he left for court.

The enthusiasm with which Cummings jumped at the chance to exonerate Rick showed Lynn not only that she was doing the right thing, but that she'd limited herself hugely by not allowing close ties in her professional or personal life. Cummings and his staff were apparently tired of fielding endless unsolicited calls and e-mails from people offering to serve as character witnesses for one Major Rick Branigan.

Rick's friends and co-workers weren't as passively accepting of his fate as he thought they were.

Lynn's cynicism crumbled completely.

But by the time she returned to her car, she knew the only tie she truly couldn't live without was her tie to Rick. At the realization, she braced her hands on the car door and hung her head to get a grip, but there was no talking herself out of her feelings.

She loved Rick. Every honorable inch of him.

No matter how long it took, or what it cost her, she had to get him to forgive her.

If only she knew how.

STARING OUT his living-room window instead of going to work as he should be, Rick couldn't shake the echo of truth in Lynn's words:

He doesn't feel any remorse. You heard him.

She was right. Not a trace of remorse could be heard in Pete's voice.

Pete had always hidden his pain by lashing out, but Rick could spot what lay beneath. And Pete had been more concerned with his own fate than that of the woman he'd hit. Because of Marissa and the baby, but still...

Are you brave enough to see for yourself the damage your friend is capable of? And if you are, while you're there, ask yourself how you'll feel the next

*time he drives drunk and someone else pays the
price.*

Was he brave enough?

He'd better be, because there was one thing Lynn
had missed: the need for an apology. The woman injured in the accident deserved an apology from someone, and seeing as he was taking responsibility, it had
to be from him.

Decision made, Rick called his lawyer to learn
where he could find Emelie Dawson. Rick's heart
plummeted when told that although she was only
forty-six, she had been moved to a nursing home
where she could receive the care and physical ther-
apy she required. Her injuries must be worse than
Rick had previously been led to believe.

Not that it mattered. She might have walked away
unscathed, but her life had still been altered when his
truck smashed into her car.

She deserved an apology.

Lynn's voice in his head said the words should be
coming from Pete, but Rick could only do what he
could do. Later, he'd find another way to help Pete
off the destructive path he'd set out on. Heaven only
knows how he'd accomplished that.

After a quick call to Carl to inform him that Rick
wouldn't be in until later that day, he drove his motorcycle to the nursing home, which was located not
far from his condo.

Or Pete's apartment.

The proximity sent a trickle of unease down his
back. To think the poor woman was lying there while

Rick and Pete went about their lives… The gravity of the situation overwhelmed Rick.

He knew what it was like to lie in a hospital bed, convalescing and wondering how much of your life you'd get back. But this woman wasn't recuperating from wounds suffered in battle or being honored for her sacrifice. She was a victim. The victim of another's criminal act.

She might not want to see Rick. He gave his name at the front desk and asked anyway. The attendant disappeared down the hall to the left, her rubber-soled shoes squeaking on the sterile linoleum. A few minutes later, she squeaked her way back.

She beckoned to him. "Right this way, Major."

Rick started, because he'd only identified himself as Rick Branigan. Then he realized she'd identified his rank from his uniform, visible beneath the partially unzipped and gaping front of his leather jacket. He hadn't thought to change before coming here. The uniform was such a part of who he was, what he was, that changing hadn't occurred to him. Losing that identity would be the hardest thing he'd ever face.

He followed the attendant to room 17C, about halfway down the hall. The room was sunny, thanks to large windows lining one wall, and the light glinted off all the stainless-steel hardware holding Emelie Dawson in traction. The bruises marring her attractive face were still dark, unlike Pete's.

The auburn-haired woman appeared tiny beneath the contraption. Her slight stature must have made her more vulnerable to the force of the airbag in her car. Of course, she hadn't been drunk like Pete, either, and had undoubtedly tensed herself right before impact, resulting in worse injuries.

She stared at him for a minute, her brow furrowed. "You're different than I remember."

Rick steeled himself. He hadn't considered for a moment that she would discern the differences between Pete and him. His hair was black to Pete's brown, and Pete was lankier.

She made a dismissing noise and looked away. "I must have been a lot more out of it than I thought. I guess excruciating pain will do that to somebody."

Regret squeezed his chest, made his voice gruff. "I'm sorry, Mrs. Dawson." He took a step forward. "That's why I'm here—to say I'm sorry this happened. That you've had to go through this." He held out a hand toward the traction device attached to the bed—and to her.

Her expression hardened. "I don't want your apology. Words that are easy to say. What I want is for you to get help, take the steps necessary to make sure you never do this to yourself or anyone else. That's all I want from you."

She pointed to her pelvis. "This is already done. It's in the past. Claiming you're sorry about it won't change a thing. But what *will* make me feel better is knowing you've learned from this. That you'll truly change your life so you'll never be tempted to drive drunk again. So that next time, someone isn't killed."

Rick's regret turned to sheer, unadulterated horror. Lynn was right. What if, next time, he found himself standing alongside a coffin instead of a hospital bed because Pete hadn't changed his ways. Sure, Pete would have to take responsibility then, but at what price?

It became excruciatingly plain to Rick that Pete should be the one standing here, seeing what his choices had wrought, hearing what his victim had to say.

Good Lord. By choosing to cover for Pete to repay the debt, Rick was grossly guilty of enabling his former best friend's drinking problem, no matter how frequent or infrequent it might be.

Emelie Dawson's face crumbled as her gaze ran over him, and tears spilled onto her battered cheeks. "Look at you." She pointed at his uniform. "You have so much to be proud of. Why would you ever want to throw it all away for a bunch of beer?"

Or on a debt owed to a man who'd never appreciate it unless he received the help he needed.

And while Pete might no longer have the Marines to lose, he had a wife and a baby coming.

Lynn had been right, about a lot of things.

Another insight stunned Rick. He'd used his overblown sense of honor to keep Lynn and her independent, self-sufficient ways at a safe distance—a distance that would ultimately cause him a lifetime of heartache and far worse regret than what he'd felt today.

Her bravery and determination and how she coped with what life threw at her drew him in a way he couldn't deny.

He was falling in love with her.

In the past, he'd used his career as an excuse not to become too deeply involved because he'd been afraid to commit to a woman. Once he did, it would be forever.

But forever still scared the crap out of him.

One step at a time, Branigan.

Blinking rapidly, he struggled to clear his own eyes, damn near overcome by his need for Lynn and the excitement and sheer terror zinging around inside him. To make it worse, he was seized by the urge to give her the one thing only he could give her.

He held up a hand. "Mrs. Dawson, I can honestly say you've changed two men's lives today. I'll come back another time to explain things further to you, but right now I need to go track down a very, very important lady."

Without giving her time to respond, Rick bolted out of the room and left the nursing home as quickly as he could without causing a disturbance. He had to find Lynn before she packed up and went back to Dependable, Missouri. He had to make sure his feelings were real.

He pulled out of the nursing home parking lot and turned his bike toward Lynn's hotel, praying that she hadn't already checked out. A big part of him seriously doubted she had, though. She wouldn't give up that easily, would she?

The memory of tears rolling down her face made him not so sure.

A car horn blaring behind him startled him back to the present. Afraid he'd unknowingly—and stupidly, considering he was on a motorcycle—cut someone off as he approached the next streetlight, he glanced over his shoulder.

Lynn. She was directly behind him, waving out the driver's window of her rental car to make sure he knew it was her. The blood and adrenaline rushing through his system were confirmation enough of his feelings for her.

At the next red light, he pulled far enough to the side that she could drive up next to him.

He flipped up the visor on his helmet. "Lynn! I—"

"I've been looking all over for you. Did you go to the nursing home to see Emelie Dawson?"

"I did. I just left her."

She hit the steering wheel with the palm of her hand. "Dang, that was going to be the last place I looked for you. I didn't think you'd really go."

"Well, I did, and I realized some pretty important stuff while I was there."

She searched his face, her amber eyes glowing with a hope tempered by a whole childhood of disappointment. "Such as?"

A white pickup truck behind them tapped his horn to let them know the light had changed to green.

Rick glanced around and spotted, of all things, a McCoy's store on the corner. He pointed at it. "Follow me there."

He pulled out in front of her and accelerated through the intersection, then turned into the large parking lot of the big-box store. He stopped in the area farthest from the doors and empty of cars.

While she parked next to him, he took off his helmet and stared up at the store's roadside sign. "Man, talk about a coincidence."

"Not really," she said as she climbed out of the car. "There's one on virtually every corner in certain markets." She leaned against the car and crossed her arms. "And trust me, anywhere near a military base is a prime market for us."

Rick nodded, but he didn't want to think about the McCoys right now, or talk about them. He could only deal with one life-altering event at a time. "Lynn, I—"

She held up a hand. "Wait a minute, Rick." She pushed off from the car and stepped close to him on the bike. "I came looking for you for a very specific reason, and I want to get it on the table before you say anything. Okay?"

He rested his forearms on the helmet in his lap. "Okay, shoot." He'd let her try to talk him over to her way of thinking before he told her he was already there. He loved watching her in action. She had an amazing mind.

"I demand you give me a chance to earn your respect."

His jaw went slack. Definitely not what he'd expected. "Lynn, you already have it."

"I—what?"

"There's no one on earth I respect more. I mean, just think about what you've overcome and what you've achieved." He lifted a hand and cupped her soft cheek. "You've even managed to get a stiff-neck like me to see beyond his own personal honor to what might be the best for everyone concerned and to recognize what he really wants for the future."

She opened her mouth, then closed it, obviously not sure what he meant.

He ran his thumb over her soft lips, wanting nothing more than to kiss them. "You know what? We shouldn't be hanging around here in some parking lot—even though I apparently own part of it. We should be making sure a former friend of mine gets the help he should have and seeing to a certain legal matter of mine that has to be cleared up. Know any good lawyers?"

Her eyebrows shot up, and he laughed, feeling freer than he'd ever felt. "Kidding. I know I couldn't get better." He cupped her face in his hands. "Especially since…I think I'm falling in love with her."

Her heart going wild in her chest, Lynn could only stare at the man she was willing to risk all for.

"Are you okay with that? Lynn?"

She closed her eyes, shutting out his beautiful, deep, warm blue ones so she could think. "I heard your words. I'm sure I did. I'm—I'm just having a little trouble processing them," she stuttered. She reached her hands up to cover his so that he wouldn't let go of her. She'd probably fall over if he did.

"Which ones are giving you the most trouble?"

The tenderness in his voice made her open her eyes again. He was gazing at her so sweetly, so lovingly, that she had to believe. But she had a lifetime of distrust to conquer. "The 'falling in love' one, of course, but mostly 'I think.' So…you're not sure?"

He moved his hand from beneath hers to brush her hair away from her face. The air felt sharp and cool on her heated cheek.

"We haven't exactly known each other that long. Or under the best of circumstances."

"No, we haven't." She laughed, embarrassed and more than a little frightened by her own certainty. But even more afraid of making any tie to Rick a reality by declaring her love for him. She desperately wanted a security that couldn't be taken away, and with him there was no guarantee.

"But I'm sure we could change that by taking a trip together, to…say, Dependable, Missouri? I hear there's going to be quite the party there sometime soon. Assuming we haven't missed it."

Utterly stunned, all she could do was stupidly answer, "No, we haven't missed it. The party isn't until July third." It dawned on her that she should be giddy with relief that he was giving her what she'd come here for—but now she wanted so much more.

She cleared her throat. "But it might take us a while to make sure you're free and clear with the authorities and arrange for your leave, since I'm sure you'll still be very much a Marine."

His expression clouded. "One with at least a letter of reprimand heading for my file for getting involved in Pete's garbage in the first place. I won't be able to advance in rank, which will effectively end my career, anyway."

"You don't know that for sure. Once they find out you were acting out of a sense of duty to Pete, your superiors might just chalk it up to you being a little too gungy."

Though a shadow remained, he laughed. "Gungy? You're sure learning a lot, aren't you."

Glowing, she smiled back at him. "Yes, I am."

He released her face and clasped her hands in his. "Well, we won't know till we know. So what do you say? Going to the party is the least I can do after all I've put you through. I want you to have that promotion, Lynn."

Her heart folded in on itself. She squeezed his hand. "I don't want you to do it for me. I want you to go because you're ready to meet the rest of your family. Because you're ready to move forward with your life and not just live it the exact opposite of how your parents lived theirs."

She loosened her hold and stared down at their hands. Hers felt so safe and secure in his. If only she could be sure it would last. "And there's something else you should know. I already took care of that 'certain legal matter' for you."

When he remained silent, she looked up at him. He was cautiously waiting for her explanation.

"I gave Pete's confession to the DA."

He inhaled deeply and shifted his gaze to the parking lot behind her. "Anonymously, I imagine."

Clearly, she had a lot to prove yet. And damn it, she would. "No. I played the recording for him myself and explained how I'd obtained it."

His eyes jerked back to hers. "But—"

"I couldn't let what happened to me happen to you, Rick. I just couldn't. It's why I went into law in the first place, but I forgot somewhere along the way."

Eyes shining with pride and understanding, he enfolded her in his embrace, holding her tight to him. "You're the honorable one, Lynn."

She clung to him, wanting to believe him, wanting to believe so many things. Only, that gut-munching fear that had driven her for so long wouldn't let her.

She fought it with everything she had.

"Come on." He eased away from her. "We have more than a few arrangements to make."

For the first time in her life, Lynn decided to take a gamble.

And trust in the power of love.

Chapter Fifteen

While she might no longer have a career to advance, on the night of July third, Lynn made sure Major Rick Branigan, the late Marcus McCoy's second oldest illegitimate son, arrived at his grandfather's seventy-fifth, black-tie birthday party right on time. A true feat, because they hadn't been able to leave Oceanedge until that very morning.

The rich, famous and influential, and those simply blessed to have fallen under Joseph's notice, were in attendance, most having come from a lot farther than quaint Dependable. The newly arrived guests, which included her and Rick, were queuing up on the steps to the magically lit, gleaming white mansion after being deposited by limos on the circular drive. Happy chatter and called greetings mingled with the music of a string quartet, set up somewhere near the front door, that filled the warm, only slightly humid evening.

Lynn had been told the party was to be a low-key affair, and she supposed it was.

By a billionaire's standards.

Wearing his "dress blues" uniform to the formal event, complete with his sword, Rick was a sight to behold among sights to behold. Lynn hadn't been able to take her eyes off him since he'd emerged from the airport restroom where he'd changed right before they met the Town Car she'd arranged to pick them up and drive them to Dependable.

With no time to swing by her apartment in town, she'd had to settle for wearing her black sheath dress again. But with Rick around, no one would be noticing her.

As they joined the people making their way through the double front doors of the McCoy mansion, thrown wide and wreathed in flowers and lights for the party, Lynn acknowledged to herself that she was more nervous now than she'd been on her first visit. She had no idea how Rick would react, and she wanted so badly for him to find some sort of connection here.

She swallowed her trepidation and leaned toward Rick. "Welcome to The Big House."

He whistled through his teeth and slipped his white, quatrefoil-hat from his head. "It makes sense, now."

On the flight east she'd done her best to fill him in on what she knew about the family and their estate, all the way down to any specifics she had on the mansion. He'd thought she'd been pulling his leg when she told him how the house—built to resemble Thomas Jefferson's domed and columned Monticello, only much larger—had been dubbed The Big House during its construction, and the nickname had stuck.

They'd barely stepped inside the huge foyer, where everyone was filing past tables laden with bouquets of flowers, sparkling punch glasses and guest books, when Lynn saw the reporter Maddy Monroe, in a stunning red-beaded dress with spaghetti straps. Next to her was her cameraman. They'd set up camp, complete with harsh glaring lights, at the foot of one of the twin curved staircases to one side of the entry, and were interviewing someone.

Rats. And she'd thought Joseph had wanted to avoid publicity until he had his new grandsons settled. Maybe he'd had to invite one in with an exclusive to keep the hordes at bay.

Lynn grabbed Rick's sleeve and pulled him to the opposite side of the foyer. "There's a reporter from *Entertainment This Evening.* I'm sure Joseph would prefer to talk to you before some reporter does."

"Why would she know who I am?"

Lynn snorted. "Because you look like a McCoy. And your red-white-and-blue stands out more than a little among all the penguin suits and ball gowns. Let's go around this way." She tugged Rick into the living room, then into a solarium. Its door led them out onto the enormous torch-lit stone veranda where most of the party was to take place. Here was the perfect spot from which to watch the fireworks Joseph was known to entertain his guests with at this time of year.

The Big House had been built on a slight rise, and thanks to the clever placement of additional torches and the subtle landscape lighting, the extensive grounds below could be seen. Beyond those were acres of rolling pasture land, hemmed on all sides by tall, white fences.

Lynn pointed at a long, low building in the distance, which could be reached from the veranda by a gently lit brick path. "Do you see that building down there?" she asked Rick.

"Mmm-hmm," he answered, but she didn't get the feeling she had his complete attention.

"That's the stable where Alexander—your oldest half brother—keeps the race horses he breeds."

Rick glanced at her. "Is that his job? Not that he needs one, I guess."

"No. He's Joseph's second-in-command at McCoy Enterprises. Alex is a truly gifted business-man. The horses are nothing more than a hobby."

He chuckled. "A rich man's hobby."

"That straight from another rich man," she reminded him. His comment was proof that the fact that he was now a part of all this hadn't sunk in yet.

He grunted in response. After a moment he said, "So how did Alex come to be raised here, as a McCoy?"

Lynn glanced around her to make sure no one was close enough to hear. No one was, so she explained. "At the time, his mother was one of the McCoys' young maids. The first woman Marcus seduced. But since he was only nineteen and dead-set against mar-riage—something that never changed—Joseph and Elise McCoy decided it would be best if they raised the baby as their own—"

"Without anyone knowing the kid wasn't theirs."

"That's right. Elise and Helen went to Europe for eight months or so and returned with a baby boy they declared to be Marcus's younger brother."

"Not his son."

"No." She'd had only glimpses of Alexander since the revelation of his parentage, and the disillusionment haunting his handsome blue eyes made her shudder. Parents could really mess you up if you let them.

"Did they pay the maid off?"

"No. Paying the women for their silence was Marcus's idea, carried out in secret, to avoid being disowned. Helen is still with the family, working as the head housekeeper. From what I can tell, she pretty much runs the household now. Elise McCoy died from cancer ten years ago."

For two and a half days, Lynn had been allowed into Joseph McCoy's inner sanctum at The Big House, to be briefed in amazing detail on the history of the family, which had turned out to be worthy of a soap opera. She still couldn't get over some of what she'd seen and learned.

Rick's dark eyebrows went up. "So she'd been picking up after this guy all that time, and he didn't know she was his mom?"

"Not a clue."

"Wow." Rick shook his head and returned to scanning the ever-growing crowd filtering out onto the veranda.

Lynn did the same, searching for Joseph McCoy's silver head. She was about to ask one of the servers if he'd seen the guest of honor, when Rick's stillness caught her attention.

He was staring at another tall, handsome, black-haired, blue-eyed man, who was staring right back. In the low light, their resemblance was uncanny, except for the length of their hair and the other man was wearing what looked to be a black Armani suit rather than dress blues.

For a second, she thought the guy was Alexander, but realized he was too young. She mused out loud, "That must be one of your half brothers."

"You don't know which?"

"No."

A pretty, petite brunette wearing an exquisite cream-colored satin gown stepped around the man and called, "Lynn!"

Sara Barnes.

Lynn grinned. "We made it, Sara," she said as she went toward the closest thing she had to a friend here in Dependable. This time when Sara hugged her she hugged back. Hard. Rick had shown her the value of friendship.

Sara leaned away and searched her face. "Is everything okay?"

Lynn couldn't keep from glancing at Rick as he joined them.

Sara's mouth formed a small O. She let go of Lynn and offered Rick her hand. "I'm Sara Barnes, vice president of operations at McCoy Enterprises. You're obviously Major Rick Branigan."

"Yes, ma'am, I am. It's a pleasure meeting you,"

Rick said with his heart-melting military polish, but Lynn could tell it was a struggle for him to keep from glancing at the other man, instead.

Ever perceptive, Sara quickly said, "Rick, may I introduce Cooper Anders, your half brother."

Cooper inclined his head and offered his hand with a wicked grin. "And Sara's fiancé."

Lynn couldn't contain her "What?"

Sara ducked her head, but her delighted smile was plain even in the dim light. "A lot has been going on since you've been gone."

"Oh, yeah," Cooper chuckled, and earned a punch in the arm from the diminutive Sara.

Rick ducked his head toward Lynn. "There must be something about finding out you're a McCoy that turns a man's thoughts to love."

Lynn did a double take, and when his words penetrated her surprise, her world exploded into tiny sparkles of pleasure.

Cooper exclaimed, "No way! You, too?" He shook Rick's hand even more enthusiastically, and at the same time called, "Hey, Mitch, we've got another live one!"

A third big man—though this one was blond and not quite as bulky, and was wearing a tan suede blazer, blue jeans and cowboy boots instead of a tux—separated himself from a nearby group of people and came toward them. He was followed by a tall fiery redhead in a simple black cocktail dress. Lynn recognized her as Alison Sullivan, the private investigator who had helped them compile as much information on the Lost Millionaires as they could in the limited amount of time they'd had.

Sara gave Lynn's hand a squeeze. "I'll go find Joseph, then we'll catch up." She patted her fiancé on the arm and slipped away.

Cooper continued talking as soon as Mitch and Alison were close. "You owe me, man. I was right. It *is* genetic."

Smiling at her and Rick, Mitch said, "Why don't you introduce us first, Cooper." But he didn't wait, offering Rick his hand. "Mitch Smith, from Whiskey Ridge, Colorado."

Rick shook his hand, his grin wide. "Rick Branigan."

That he left off "United States Marine Corps" broke Lynn's heart.

Mitch tipped an imaginary hat. "Pleasure to meet you, Major."

"To be honest," Rick said, "I didn't think I'd care when I first found out, but now that I'm here, it really is a pleasure to meet both of you, too."

Hit by a powerful desire for a connection—a family—of her own, Lynn felt her happiness for Rick turn bittersweet.

Mitch clasped his shoulder and squeezed. "We know exactly what you mean, brother." He released Rick and planted his hands on his hips. "I myself am only a couple hours into the McCoy Experience. But I'm sure that together we'll navigate through just fine."

"I'd like that," Rick said. "I'd like that a lot."

A booming voice reached them. "Where is my last grandson?"

Cooper raised his hand and hailed, "Grandpa Joe!"

But Lynn knew that even if there was anything wrong with Joseph McCoy's eyesight, which there wasn't, he'd have a hard time missing this bunch.

Beside her, Rick stood taller, his shoulders squared, a wary tension in his jaw.

The eldest McCoy made his way toward them in his black tuxedo, tall and strong despite his age.

Rick threw his arms wide, his tension visibly broken as he welcomed his grandfather's hug.

Tears flooded Lynn's eyes. She couldn't be happier for him. Ties were already being formed through simple kinship, and she knew how important it was for Rick to be a part of something. If he couldn't have the Marines, maybe the mighty McCoys would fill the void.

Joseph finally released him. "Rick, my boy. My Marine."

Rick said, "Not for long, I'm afraid, sir."

Joseph made a dismissive noise. "Don't despair yet. There might still be compromises to reach. And assuming the best, I want you to know right off that the terms of Marcus's will—the ones regarding you taking your place in the family business—can wait until you retire from the Marines. Our country needs men like you. A McCoy never sends up the white flag."

Rick stared at Joseph for a moment. Finally, a slow grin spread across his handsome face. "Sir, yes, sir."

Joseph clapped a hand on Rick's shoulder, then pulled him into an embrace again. "Thank you.

Thank you for being here and making an old man's wish come true."

When Joseph finally released him, Rick reached for Lynn's hand and drew her near.

Included her.

Tender, tentative joy flooded her veins, warming her with hope. Her heart felt as if it were about to burst, he filled it up so much.

Rick squeezed her hand. "This amazing woman right here deserves the credit."

Joseph beamed. "Is that so?"

Lynn had to be honest. Rick deserved nothing less. "Actually, Rick, I don't. Your grandfather made it possible for you to leave. He'd already arranged for you to plead 'no contest' to a lesser charge and serve your probation with him here in Dependable."

Rick's dark eyebrows slammed together. "Before you turned in Pete's confession?"

"Yes."

He brought her hand up to his chest. "Then why did you risk your career that way?"

She smiled at him through her tears and drew courage from what he'd taught her. That the only real security, the kind that couldn't be taken away, was in committing to someone heart and soul. "Because you mean more to me, Rick. More than my career."

Painfully aware of their audience, she hesitated to say more.

Joseph whispered, "Go on, girl, tell him. It's all in the family now, anyhow."

Lynn laughed and nodded. She liked the sound of that. Ties didn't limit after all. They made her feel safe, secure and loved. "I suppose you're right."

She pulled in a shuddering breath and focused on Rick. Only Rick. "I did it because I love you, Rick. I know you need more time to be sure, but—"

He swept her up into his arms, his cheek pressed against hers. "That's what you think," he murmured. "I love you and I want forever with you, Lynn. Forever and ever."

There was nothing tentative about the euphoria sweeping through her, making her light-headed.

Next thing she knew, Joseph was hugging them both.

When he stepped back, allowing them to separate, the head of the powerful McCoys and one of the richest men in the nation had tears in his eyes. "Now my life is complete." He spread his arms in an expansive gesture. "Those who remain of my family are with me—" He stopped and brought his thick silver brows together. "Where's Alexander?"

Worry rippled through the group.

Sara rejoined them, and stood next to Lynn.

Lynn asked her in a whisper, "What's going on with Alex?"

Sara answered in kind. "He's not taking this well. He's happy for these guys—" she nodded at the freshly acquainted half brothers "—but he's not sure how to handle his new relationship with Joseph."

Lynn murmured agreement. Nothing like going

from being someone's youngest son to being his eldest grandson to mess with a man's head.

Cooper leaned in to ask Sara something, and Lynn found herself being drawn away from everyone by a handsome man in uniform.

Rick pulled her into his arms again. "Miss Hayes, I want to make one thing clear to you before there are any more distractions."

He dropped his head until his forehead rested against hers. "I'm damn sure I love *you,* Lynn. I swear you'll never regret taking a risk loving me."

Certain she was the luckiest woman in the world, she slipped her arms around his neck and pulled his lips toward hers. "Coming from a man of honor like you, I think I'm good."

* * * * *

Spring in the Valley (#1061) is the third book in Charlotte Douglas's popular series A PLACE TO CALL HOME. The previous titles are *Almost Heaven* and *One Good Man*.

When you read *Spring in the Valley,* you'll meet local police officer Brynn Sawyer and New York City attorney Rand Benedict, who's come to Pleasant Valley with his orphaned nephew. Brynn and Rand quickly develop a relationship—but Rand has a secret agenda that's going to affect not only Brynn but the whole town. Still, Rand will find himself enchanted by Pleasant Valley…. It's the kind of place where neighbors become friends and where people care—small-town life as it was meant to be!

Hiking her long silk skirt above her boots, Officer Brynn Sawyer slid from the car and used her Mag-Lite to guide her steps to the idling Jaguar she'd pulled over. At her approach, the driver's window slid down with an electronic whir.

The driver started to speak. "I have a—"

"I'll do the talking. This is a state highway, not a NASCAR track," Brynn said in the authoritative manner she reserved for lawbreakers, especially those displaying such an obvious lack of common sense. "And the road's icing up. You have a death wish?"

"No." The driver seemed distracted, oblivious to the seriousness of his offense. "I need to—"

"Turn off your engine," Brynn ordered, "and place your hands on the wheel where I can see them."

She shined her flashlight in the driver's face. The man, who was in his midthirties, squinted in the brightness, but not before the pupils of his eyes, the color of dark melting chocolate, contracted in the light. She instantly noted the rugged angle of his unshaven jaw, the aristocratic nose, baby-fine brown hair tousled as if he'd just climbed out of bed...

And a wad of one-hundred-dollar bills thrust under her nose.

Anger burned through her, but she kept her temper. "If that's a bribe, buster, you're in a heap of trouble."

"No bribe." His tone, although frantic, was rich and full. "Payment for my fine. I can't stop—"

"You can't keep going at your previous speed either," she said reasonably and struggled to control her fury at the man's arrogance. "You'll kill yourself and someone else—"

"It's Jared. I have to get him to the hospital."

Labored breathing sounded in the back seat. Brynn aimed her light at the source. In a child carrier, a tow-headed toddler, damp hair matted to his head and plump cheeks flushed with fever, wheezed violently as his tiny chest struggled for air.

Brynn's anger vanished at the sight of the poor little guy, and her sympathy kicked in. She made a quick decision.

"Follow me. I'll radio ahead for the E.R. to expect us."

With *Discovering Duncan* (#1062), Mary Anne Wilson launches a brand-new four-book series, RETURN TO SILVER CREEK. In these stories, various characters return to a Nevada town for a variety of reasons—to hide, to come home, to confront their pasts. In *Discovering Duncan,* a young private detective, Lauren Carter, is hired to track down a wealthy client's son. When she does so, she also discovers the person he really is—not to mention the delights of this small mountain town!

"I'm a man of patience," D. R. Bishop said as his secretary left, closing the door securely behind her. "But even I have my limits."

Lauren Carter never took her eyes off the large man across from her at the impressive stone and glass desk. D. R. Bishop was dressed all in black. He was a huge, imposing man, and definitely, despite what he said, a man with little patience. He looked tightly wound, and ready to spring.

Lauren sat very still in a terribly uncomfortable chair, her hands in her lap while she let D. R. Bishop do all the talking. She simply nodded from time to time.

"My son walked out on everything six months ago," he said.

"Why?"

He tented his fingers thoughtfully, with his elbows resting on the polished desktop, as if he were considering her single-word question. But she knew he was considering just how much to tell her. His eyes were dark as night, a contrast to his snow-white hair and meticulously trimmed beard. "Ah, that's a good question," he said. For some reason, he was hedging.

"Mr. Bishop, you've dealt with the Sutton Agency enough to know that privacy and discretion are part of our service. Nothing you tell me will go any further."

He shrugged his massive shoulders and sank back in his chair. "Of course. I expect no less," he said.

"So, why did your son leave?"

"I thought it was a middle-age crisis of some sort." He smiled slightly, a strained expression. "Not that thirty-eight is middle-aged. Then I thought he might be having a breakdown. Maybe gone over the edge." The man stood abruptly, rising to his full, imposing height, and she could've sworn she felt the air ripple around her from his movement. "But he's not crazy, Ms. Carter, he's just damn stubborn. Too damn stubborn."

She waited as he walked to the windows behind him and faced the city twenty floors below. When he didn't speak, she finally said, "You don't know why he left?"

The shoulders shrugged again. "A difference of opinion on how to do business. Nothing new for us."

He spoke without turning. "We've always clashed, but in the end, we've always managed to make our business relationship work."

"What exactly do you want from the Sutton Agency, Mr. Bishop?"

"Find him."

"That's it?"

He turned back to her, studying her intently for several moments before he said, "No."

"Then what else do you want us to do?"

"As an employee of Sutton, I want you to find my son. I also want him to come back willingly."

"Okay," she said. She'd handle it. She had to. Her future depended on finding the mysterious Duncan Bishop.

We're thrilled to introduce a brand-new writer to American Romance! *Mad About Max* (#1063) is the first of three books by Penny McCusker. They're set in Erskine, Montana, where the residents gather at the Ersk Inn to trade gossip and place bets in the watering hole's infamous betting pools. Cute, klutzy schoolteacher Sara Lewis is the current subject of one of the inn's most popular pools ever. She's been secretly (or not so secretly!) pining for rancher and single dad Max Devlin for going on six years, and this story sees her about to take her destiny into her own hands.

Penny writes with the perfect mix of warmth and humor, and her characters will have you cheering for them right to the end.

"Please tell me that wasn't Super Glue."

Sara Lewis tore her gaze away from the gorgeous—and worried—blue eyes of Max Devlin, looking up to where her hands were flattened against the wall over his head. Even when she saw the damning evidence squished between her right palm and her third-grade class's mangled Open House banner, she refused to admit it, even to herself.

If she admitted she was holding a drained tube of Super Glue in her hand, she might begin to wonder if there'd been any stray drops. And where they might have landed. That sort of speculation would only lead her to conclusions she'd be better off not drawing, conclusions like there was no way a stray drop could have landed on the floor. Not with her body plastered to Max's. No, that kind of speculation would lead her right into trouble.

As if she could have gotten into any more trouble.

She'd been standing on a chair, putting up the banner her third-grade class had created to welcome their parents to Erskine Elementary's open house. But her hands had jerked when she heard Max's voice out in the hallway, and she'd torn it clear in half. She'd grabbed the first thing off her desk that might save the irreplaceable strip of laboriously scrawled greetings and brilliant artwork and jumped back on her chair, only to find that Max had gotten there first. He'd grabbed one end of the banner, then dived for the other as it fluttered away, ending up spread-eagled against the wall, one end of the banner in either hand, trapped there by Sara and her chair.

She'd pulled the ragged ends of the banner together, but just as she'd started to glue them, Max had turned around and nearly knocked her over. "Hold still," she'd said sharply, not quite allowing herself to notice that he was facing her now, that perfect male body against hers, that heart-stopping face only inches away. Instead, she'd asked him to hold the banner in place while she applied the glue. The rest was history. Or in her case infamy.

"Uh, Sara…" Max was trying to slide out from between her and the wall, but she met his eyes again and shook her head.

"Uh, just hold on a little longer, Max. I want to make sure the glue is dry."

What she really needed was a moment to figure out how badly she'd humiliated herself this time. Experimentally, she stuck out her backside. Sure enough, the front of her red pleather skirt tented dead center, stuck fast to the lowermost pearl button on Max's shirt—the button that was right above his belt buckle, which was right above his—

Sara slammed her hips back against his belly, an automatic reaction intended to halt the dangerous direction of her thoughts and hide the proof of her latest misadventure. It was like throwing fuel on the fire her imagination had started.

Blood rushed into her face, then drained away to throb deep and low, just about where his belt buckle was digging into her—

"Sara!"

She snapped back to reality, noting the exasperation in his voice, reluctantly she arched away from him. The man had to breathe, after all.

"There's a perfectly reasonable explanation for this," she said in a perfectly reasonable voice. In fact, that voice amazed her, considering that she was glued to a man she'd been secretly in love with for the better part of six years.

"There always is, Sara," Max said, exasperation giving way to amusement. "There was a perfectly reasonable explanation for how Mrs. Tilford's cat wound up on top of the church bell tower."

Sara grimaced.

"There was a perfectly reasonable explanation for why Jenny Hastings went into the Crimp 'N Cut a blonde and came out a redhead. Barn-red."

Sara cringed.

"And there was a perfectly reasonable explanation for the new stained-glass window in the town hall looking more like an advertisement for a brothel than a reenactment of Erskine's founding father rescuing the Indian maidens."

She huffed out a breath, indignant. "I only broke the one pane."

"Yeah, the pane between the grateful, kneeling maidens and the very happy Jim 'Mountain Man' Erskine."

"The talk would die down if the mayor let me get the pane fixed instead of just shoving the rest of them together so it looked like the Indian maidens were, well, really grateful."

"People are coming from miles around to see it." Max reminded her. "He'd lose the vote of every businessman in town if he ruined the best moneymaker they've ever had."

Sara just huffed out another breath. It was a little hypocritical for the people of Erskine, Montana, to pick on her for something they were capitalizing on, especially when she had a perfectly good reason for

why it had happened, why bad luck seemed to follow her around like a black cloud. Except she
couldn't tell anyone what that reason was, especially
not Max. Because he was the reason.

Veteran author Ginger Chambers returns to American Romance with *Love, Texas,* a warm, engrossing story about returning to your past—coming home—and seeing it in an entirely new way…. You'll enjoy Ginger's determined and delightful heroine, Cassie Edwards, and her rancher hero, Will Taylor. Cassie is more and more drawn into life at the Taylor ranch—and you will be, too. Guaranteed you'll feel right at home in Love, Texas!

When Cassie Edwards arrived at the Four Corners—where Main Street was intersected by Pecan—nothing in Love, Texas, seemed to have changed. At Swanson's Garage the same old-style gasoline pumps waited for customers under the same rickety canopy. The Salon of Beauty still sported the same eye-popping candy-pink front door. Handy Grocery & Hardware's windows were plastered with what could be the same garish sale banners. And from the number of pickup trucks and cars crowded into the parking lot on the remaining corner, Reva's Café still claimed the prize as the area's most popular eating place.

Old feelings of panic threatened to engulf Cassie,

forcing her to pull the car onto the side of the road. She had to remember she wasn't the same Cassie Edwards the people of Love thought they knew so well. She'd changed.

Cassie gripped the steering wheel. She'd come here to do a job—to negotiate a land deal, get the needed signatures, then get out...fast!

A flutter of unease went through her as her thoughts moved to her mother, but she quickly beat it down. She'd known all along that she'd have to see her. But the visit would be brief and it would be the last thing she did before starting back for Houston. She glanced in the rearview mirror and pulled back out onto Main and continued toward the Taylor ranch.

Cassie drove down the highway, following a line of tightly strung barbed wire that enclosed grazing Black Angus cattle. The working fence ran for about a mile before being replaced by a rustic rock fence that decorated either side of a wide metal gate, on which the ranch's name, the Circle Bar-T, was proudly displayed in a circle of black wrought-iron. A sprawling two-story white frame house with a wraparound porch sat a distance down the driveway, the rugged landscape around it softened with flowers and more delicate greenery.

Cassie hopped out of the car, swung open the gate and drove through.

"Hey!" a man shouted.

Cassie looked around and saw a jeans-clad man in a long-sleeved shirt and bone-colored hat heading toward her, and he didn't look pleased. She'd had a thing for Will Taylor when she'd first started to notice boys. Trim and athletic with thick blond hair and eyes the same blue as the Texas sky, he was handsome in the way that made a girl's heart quicken if he so much as looked at her. But even if he had noticed her in the same way she'd noticed him, there'd been a gulf between them far wider than the difference in their ages. She was Bonnie Edwards's daughter. And that was enough.

"You forgot somethin', ma'am," he drawled. "You didn't close the gate. In these parts if you open a gate, you need to close it."

Will Taylor continued to look at her. Was he starting to remember her, too?

He broke into her thoughts. "Just go knock on the front door. My mom's expectin' you." Then, with a little nod, he stuffed his hat back on his head and walked away.

Cassie stared after him. Not exactly an auspicious beginning.

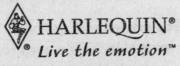

Harlequin Romance®

Contract Brides

From paper marriage...to wedded bliss?

A *wedding dilemma*:

What should a sexy, successful bachelor do if he's too busy making millions to find a wife? Or if he finds the perfect woman, and just has to strike a bridal bargain...?

The *perfect proposal*:

The solution? For better, for worse, these grooms in a hurry have decided to sign, seal and deliver the ultimate marriage contract...to buy a bride!

Coming soon to

HARLEQUIN®
Romance®

in the favorite miniseries Contract Brides:

VACANCY: WIFE OF CONVENIENCE
by Jessica Steele, #3839
on sale April 2005

HIS HIRED BRIDE
by Susan Fox, #3848
on sale June 2005

Available wherever Harlequin books are sold.

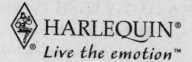